KT-445-158

WHITE
LIES

ABOUT THE AUTHOR

Mark O'Sullivan is a writer whose work has won several awards in Ireland and France and has been translated into six languages. He is married with two daughters and lives in County Tipperary.

WHITE LIES

MARK O'SULLIVAN

Little Island

This edition published 2010
by Little Island
An imprint of New Island
2 Brookside
Dundrum Road
Dublin 14

www.littleisland.ie

First published in Ireland in 1997 by Wolfhound Press Ltd.

Copyright © Mark O'Sullivan 1997

The author has asserted his moral rights.

ISBN 978-1-84840-942-2

All rights reserved. The material in this publication is protected by copyright law. Except as may be permitted by law, no part of the material may be reproduced (including by storage in a retrieval system) or transmitted in any form or by any means; adapted; rented or lent without the written permission of the copyright owner.

British Library Cataloguing Data. A CIP catalogue record for this book is available from the British Library.

Cover design by Fidelma Slattery.

Inside design by Sinéad McKenna.

Printed by ColourBooks Ltd Ireland

Little Island received financial assistance from
The Arts Council (An Chomhairle Ealaíon), Dublin, Ireland.
10 9 8 7 6 5 4 3 2 1

For Joan, Jane and Ruth

Also by Mark O'Sullivan

Children's fiction
Melody for Nora
Washbasin Street Blues
More than a Match

Young Adult Fiction
Angels Without Wings
Silent Stones

Adult Fiction
Enright

NANCE

I suppose you could call it delayed shock. It had been two weeks since I'd found the photo, and my life had gone on as normal. At least, that's how it must have seemed to OD, my boyfriend, and to everyone else. But inside I'd gone numb. I couldn't think, I couldn't study. I felt nothing. And then I cracked.

The child in the photo was me. I was certain of it. My brown skin, the tight black curls, something about the eyes. I don't know how long I spent there, gaping at the photo, before I put it back exactly where I found it; but, to this day, I can remember every detail of it. The impossibly blue sky, the lush green trees in the background, the bright colours of their clothes. There were five adults in the photo. My adoptive mother, May, stood young and fresh-faced between a man and woman, two real hippy types who looked like they hadn't slept for a month. But it was the pair in front who really grabbed my attention. I didn't have to look twice to be sure that here, holding the tiny black infant, was my natural mother. Then there was the man crouched beside her. Tall, and darker than I am, but with my eyes. My father. I was certain of it.

The strange thing about the photo was that none of them were smiling except for the woman who held me. This convinced me even more that she really was my natural mother.

Tom and May had always told me that they never knew my natural parents.

The first thing I felt, before I stopped feeling anything at all, was guilt for having discovered the photo at the back of Tom and May's wardrobe. It wasn't the first time I'd searched in there among May's old clothes, the kind of stuff that's back in fashion again – flares, Adidas wear. May never throws anything out. But, knowing I often went through her things, why did she leave the photo there? It's not the kind of thing you forget, is it? And the blonde woman in the photo, the woman holding the baby? I'd never seen her before, but I guessed she was the same one May had gone to Kenya with as a young teacher in 1975. Heather. Heather Kelly. May had only ever mentioned her once or twice in passing and I never asked questions. In fact, I rarely asked about that distant part of my life. I think I felt deep down that if I did, I'd discover things I wasn't ready to know.

Besides, I had no reason to doubt the story as I knew it. Tom had gone out to Kenya in 1977 and joined the staff at

May's school outside Nairobi. They married early in 1979. A few months before they left for Ireland, later that same year, they adopted me. I was the child, they said, of a mixed-race marriage and my parents had died in a car crash.

More than once, OD had told me he was surprised I never wanted to find out more about myself. I just told him I knew who I was, but it always felt like a lie. And lies can be easy to live with if you bury them deep enough. I buried mine beneath a heavy schedule of study, sport – and going out with OD.

I didn't have much time left to think about how different I was. But whether I liked to admit it or not, I was different. I was the only coloured person in a town of seven thousand, which is as different as you can get, I suppose. But I was sure that was as far as it went. In every other way I was the same as everyone else, and I was rarely made to feel anything but one of the crowd. Whenever I was reminded, I never felt humiliated – why should I? What I felt was anger. And, besides, I had plenty of defenders if I needed them.

Like the time a gang of us were in the back room of the Galtee Lounge watching Ireland play in a World Cup qualifier. There were eight of us there but only a few were drinking: Johnny Regan – a pimply drughead and general rat – and, of course, OD. I still thought then that I could straighten OD out, that I just had to wait and be patient.

Johnny worked with OD on the FÁS Scheme, building the new town park. When Paul McGrath's bad clearance early on led to a goal, Johnny hit the roof.

'You black bastard!' he roared. Everyone looked at me. Except Johnny, who was too smashed to notice.

I picked up his pint glass and emptied the Guinness over his greasy head. OD caught him by the scruff of the neck and, with his crazy pal Beano's help, bundled Johnny out the back door.

Johnny didn't hang around us after that, but he got his own back when things began to go wrong between OD and me.

But, as I said, these things didn't happen very often. When they did, I always ended up feeling people were on my side, so I could forget quickly. With the Leaving Cert coming up in less than three months I had even less time than usual to wonder about who I was. And there was OD to worry about. He was making a mess of his life, and I was wondering what I could do to make him see sense.

Then, on Monday, the fourth of April, I found the photo. I often think it should have happened three days before. The first of April. Fools' Day.

Two weeks later, I sat by a roaring fire in our sitting room. May and Tom had gone out, as they usually did on Sunday nights, to meet some friends. OD had been up earlier and wanted me to go out celebrating his team's win over St. Peter's in the Youths League.

Don't get me wrong. I like soccer. But when your boyfriend is on the town's Youths team and your father – your adoptive father – is the manager you can get a bit tired of football talk.

OD was on a high. St. Peter's had been two points ahead of them going into the game and he'd scored the winner.

'Couldn't we go to the pictures?' I said.

I knew something was going to happen that night because I'd started thinking again. I was feeling things I'd been avoiding for two weeks. I didn't want to talk to anyone or pretend everything was rosy. OD should have realised I wasn't myself, but he let me down. I needed the comfort of silence; he wanted the comfortable blur of noise. It was the beginning of the end.

'You want to see *The Bodyguard*,' he sneered unpleasantly. 'Again!'

It was an old joke – white boy saves black girl – and I didn't like it.

'We could get a video and stay in.'

'Tom can't stand the sight of me, you know that. He'd freak out if he caught me here.'

'We've stayed in before and he never complained.'

'Maybe he doesn't say anything, but I know how he looks at me. He couldn't wait to see the back of me out of that dump of a school. Soon as he gets a chance, he'll have me off the team, too.'

'You didn't need any excuses to leave school, OD.'

Then the usual vicious argument started up – me telling him he was throwing everything away and him telling me that anything was better than the hassle from teachers, especially Tom, who's the vice-principal at our Community

College.

OD had never been what you'd call the studious type. Always too busy with soccer, rugby, hurling – and messing. Still, he'd always managed to be in the top five in our class, and in the Junior Cert his results weren't far short of my seven A's and two B's. It seemed to come so easily to him. But in fifth year he started to slip. Then I started going out with him and found out what was up.

His parents hadn't been getting on. His mother had just gone to England and left OD and his father, Jimmy, in a state of disbelief that soon turned to anger on OD's part – anger not towards his mother but towards Jimmy and everyone else around him. And towards himself, of course.

Soon, he packed in school. I couldn't get him to see he was punishing himself for someone else's mistakes. But I couldn't walk away from him, not at a time like that. And besides, I liked being with him. He was tall, dark and wide-eyed, and something was always happening when he was around. If it wasn't, he made something happen. He could be funny when you wanted a laugh and serious when you were in a mood to talk.

When he got drunk it was a different story. I don't know whether it was a case of me being blind or him being careful, but it was months before I realised he drank too much. Maybe it was the fact that instead of getting rowdy, like you'd expect, he'd just go quiet. As time went on, he drank more and more when I was around, as if my silence was some kind of acceptance, and I began to notice that this quietness had nothing to do with calm. More and more I could sense this aura of nervous, pent-up energy in him, like he was clenching his brain as hard as he clenched his fists. That was when the bitter jokes, like the *Bodyguard* one, came out. And there was something else too. The tension I felt when he got like that was exactly what I felt after a dream I'd had, from time to time, ever since I can remember.

In the dream I seem to be very young and small and I'm hiding in a dark place. I can see nothing but I know something bad is happening outside my hideaway. I can hear the sounds of an argument but can't recognise the voices. The dream ends with a loud bang. When I wake, the sweat is pouring from me. The same fear hit me when OD got like that. That's when the real doubt began to set in and I realised that I'd never really get inside that muddled head of his.

Beano – Brendan Doyle, OD's friend – had his own theory.

'He reads too many books,' he'd tell me. 'I saw him reading a poetry book one time. Not for school, like. He actually bought the thing!'

But back to that Sunday night. We ended up, as usual, with a few last taunts. 'What's on telly, anyway, only crap,' he said. Then, another cut: 'Crap like *The Cosby Show*.'

Another bitter old joke – I was the comfortable middle-class black, just like the Cosbys; he was the poor white boy.

'So, what programme do you fit into? *Home and Away*?' I

7

asked dismissively.

I should have known he'd have a smart answer ready.

'*Only Fools and Horses*,' he said. 'Without the jokes.'

'Get lost, OD. Go and drink yourself silly. Pretend you're alive.'

'Don't talk to me like that.'

'You like talking tough, don't you?'

'It's your fault. You're driving me to it, Nance.'

'It's always someone else's fault with you, isn't it?'

His mind was working overtime but there were no more smart answers coming through. He gave up trying.

'I'm out of here,' he muttered and swayed a little as he went to the sitting-room door.

Out in the hallway, his hand somehow got tangled in the telephone cord as he passed by. When he tried to get free, the phone fell to the ground.

'See what you made me do,' he said. He didn't even bother to pick it up.

I closed the front door behind him without a word and went back into the sitting room. I opened the geography book I'd been studying before he'd called. OD had given it to me when he'd walked out of school. His initials were still on the front cover.

I flicked through the pages. I got to the chapter on Africa and my finger slowly followed the outline of that continent until it came to Kenya. I tore out the page with venom, crumpled it up and threw it in the fire. I did the same with every other page in the book. Then I ripped the cover to pieces and watched as the flames encircled the initials, 'OD', and swallowed them up, and the frail black remains fell asunder among the red-hot coals.

The maths book came next. I love maths – you can find such predictable, tidy answers – but maths wasn't going to help with this problem. European history followed, then Irish history, accountancy, every textbook I could find. The last one was an English book. Tom was my English teacher.

Then I started with my notes. *Macbeth*, the poetry ... and the chimney began to roar out with a deep bellow I could feel in the pit of my stomach.

Great lumps of steaming black gunge fell on to the hearth. I ran outside to the front lawn and saw flames shooting out of the chimney pot. Curtains moved in the houses opposite and I screamed out, 'Mind your own business!'

I went back inside and rang the fire brigade.

'What's the problem?' the woman at the other end of the line asked.

'Fire,' I said foolishly. 'Send someone to help me.'

OD

I loved weekend nights. I always had enough money to spend, and that made me feel I was better off out of school. If there was something to celebrate, like beating St. Peter's and scoring the winner, it was even better. All night I'd never think that I'd be broke and hungover in the morning. For some reason I can't remember, our game was moved from Saturday to Sunday that weekend. After the match, I was up for a good time and Nance was being awkward. She made a habit of that. When I think about it, the reason I liked her and the reason she got on my nerves were basically the same. She had a mind of her own, a kind of cool, independent spirit that made her stand out from everyone else.

When she'd get on to me about leaving school and all that stuff, there was something cold and sarcastic about the way she talked. It was like she was warning me she wasn't going to hang around forever with someone who had no future. I hated that. I'd sort of cut my mind off and get thick. She had a way past that too. She'd make me feel like this mindless primitive, ready at any minute to lash out – even at her. It was true that there were a few people I wouldn't have minded belting, but that was all in my head, and I was sure it was going to stay there.

That business of me knocking over the phone was typical. The way she looked at me! You'd swear I'd meant to do it. I didn't pick the phone up because I knew if I did I'd throw it through the glass on the front door.

The funny thing was, I started going out with her just to get back at her old man. I'd got on fine with him until things started to go wrong at home – I should say, when the things that were already wrong started coming out into the open. Tom Mahoney put the boot into me when I came in once too often with nothing done. No way was I going to tell him I lived in a war zone that was worse when they went quiet than when they were screaming at each other. First day back in September, he lays it on the line for me. I had three weeks to prove to him I could take the honours paper. I told him where to shove it and things went from worse to horrific. At the end of the three weeks I said goodbye to the place. A week later, Mahoney took over as manager of the Youths team. I should have known then that you can't run away. That hating Mahoney was just an excuse.

So I asked Nance for a dance at a disco shortly after. I wasn't talking to her for more than five minutes before I'd forgotten all about Mahoney. Before the night was out I'd

11

told her everything. All that stuff about my folks and the hassle with Mahoney. She didn't lead me on or ask questions, but somehow she drew it all out of me. It was like I'd been waiting for the right person to listen.

My father was an alcoholic. He was coming up to his fiftieth birthday: a failed musician, a failed husband, a failed father. He'd spent his early days playing trumpet in the showbands and doing really well. For a while, he was near the top with a band called the New Mexicanos. We used to have two copies of an old music magazine called *Spotlight* at home and he's smiling out of some photographs there. He's dressed up in a daft sombrero hat and black velvet suit, embroidered along the lapels with gold braid. I showed them to Beano once. I don't know why.

'You're the spittin' image of him!' he said. That freaked me out. I hunted Beano home and I never looked at the things again.

Anyway, the showband scene in Ireland started to fall apart when discos came in. It was the end of the road for the New Mexicanos and a lot of other bands. We moved to Dublin for a year and my old man tried to get into the jazz scene there, but it didn't work out. I think this hurt much harder than the collapse of the New Mexicanos. Jazz was the 'real music' as far as he was concerned. That's how I got my name. I was called after two old jazz greats. The O is for Oliver – King Oliver. The D, believe it or not, is Dizzy – Dizzy Gillespie. When I was a kid they called me Oliver, or worse, Ollie. I came up with the OD myself when I was about twelve. Dizzy would have suited better because that was me – permanently dizzy. Anyway, we came back to town and he played the pubs with a mate of his for seven or eight years. The drinking got worse. Then his friend died of a heart attack. Jimmy never got over that.

He sold his trumpet and drank the money in a week. It was forty-five pounds, I still remember that. He gave Mam a fiver. I got a pound. He borrowed it back from me at the end of the week and I never heard a word about it again.

The truth was, he was finished long before his friend died. He'd got this gum disease and the few teeth he had left had to be taken out. You can't blow a trumpet without teeth, so he got a false set. They worked all right for a while, but in the end he couldn't put up with the pain of the plastic, or whatever it is, clamped to his raw gums – so he told us, anyway. I reckon it was true, because the day he sold the trumpet, he took out the false teeth and left them out. It made him look even older than before.

That was when Mam gave up on him. I wasn't able to say it before she left, but I knew she'd tried her best. She even got odd jobs to pay for the extras I needed at school. There was never a word of thanks. Not from him. Not from me. So maybe I didn't deserve to be warned. But she'd gone through the hard bit, the deciding to go; surely saying goodbye to me wouldn't have killed her? Then again, I should have known. The night before she went she talked to me about him for the first and last time. I mean really talked about him. Not ripping him apart, as she had every right to do, but about how they met and how good the early days were.

It was during his New Mexicanos days. He was already thirty but he didn't look it. She was seventeen. It was her first dance. My old man comes to the mike to do a vocal. An old Elvis song, she said: 'The Wonder of You'. When she started humming it softly I didn't know where to look, but I listened. It was as close to her as I ever got in those last days.

She was a million miles away, then, from the screaming arguments and that horrible night when they actually came to blows. I don't know who hit who first but, though I was twelve years old, I wet the bed that night. I wouldn't let either of them change the sheets. I did it myself and for a week after. This was one part of that ugly story of my childhood I held back from Nance. It just wouldn't come out. If it had, maybe Nance would have understood how I could never hit her, not in a million years.

All that stuff was far from my mind as I watched Mam that night. There were no tears. She wasn't like that happy girl any more but she didn't seem bitter either. That was when I should have known.

'Before he got to the end of the song,' she said, 'I was ... well, I was head over heels. I thought he was the most fantastic looking fellow I'd ever seen. He looked like you do now.'

I thought I'd break up when I heard that, but I held it in.

I was good at that, holding stuff in. Which I don't recommend, because when that stuff spills out you're into disaster territory, believe me.

On the night of our celebrations after the St. Peter's game I was still holding it all in. Just about.

Beano walked me home from the Galtee Lounge, ready to catch me if I fell and persuading me not to call up to Nance's house. It was nearly one o'clock in the morning. I thought I was being perfectly reasonable. If it wasn't for him I'd have dug myself into twice as many holes as I've done in my time.

Beano was eighteen and we'd been best friends for going on nine years. He was small for his age and he was an albino – white hair, chalk-white skin and red-tinged eyes. We'd met up in third class in primary school. He'd already stayed back a year because he couldn't keep up. We got as far as fifth class together and then he was kept back again – and again. He finished primary when he was fourteen and gave it up as a bad job. We stayed friends through all this, and for years I was his protector – until he had to become mine.

Beano's father is Snipe Doyle, who was foreman at the FÁS Scheme when we built the town park. He didn't like me. Which is putting it mildly. Then again, he didn't like anyone very much – not even Beano. If there was some messy, back-breaking job at the site that no-one fancied doing, chances were me and Beano got it. Beano would go all silent when I'd bring this up. No matter what Snipe did or said to him, he hadn't a bad word to say about his old man.

That Sunday night, Beano finally got me to the front gate of my house. Then he had to put up with a poetry recitation. I'd just learned off Dylan Thomas's 'The Force That through the Green Fuse'. I hadn't much of an idea of what it was about, but the words sounded so good, they wouldn't leave me alone. It was like there was this language that said everything about life and if you tried hard enough you could understand it and begin to see through the clouds of crap all around you.

After a lot of persuasion, I dragged myself inside and found Jimmy sleeping on his grotty armchair in front of a fireplace full of dead ashes. His head was back, cushioned by his lank, shoulder-length hair. His toothless mouth was open. I sat in a chair opposite him and stared until he came to.

The last thing I expected was the wide grin he gave me when he woke. The offer to make me a cup of tea nearly knocked me flat. I didn't answer him. He stood up and walked straight as a die to the kitchen sink to fill the kettle. I couldn't understand why he wasn't drunk. In fact, it had been a few months since I'd actually seen him in that state. Then again, he was usually in bed by the time I got home, so that didn't mean anything.

'I heard you scored a right one today,' he said, as he waited for the kettle to boil.

He never talked about football. I was sobering up fast.

'How come you weren't out tonight?' I asked. 'Spent it all last night, I suppose.'

He shook his head and that dumb smile appeared again. I took it personally.

'What's the stupid grin for? You think I'm funny when I'm drunk, you should see yourself.'

'I have, OD, I have.'

The tea was weak and soapy like it always was in our house. I drank it anyway. I needed an excuse to stay up and find out what was going on. Eventually, he came out with it.

'I was down town after dinner and I met a fellow I haven't seen for years,' he began. I stared at the white, powdery rim of lime at the top of my cup. His saintly smile was getting to me.

'This bloody big green BMW pulls up beside me and I'm thinking this has to be somebody I owe money to. Then he stops and jumps out, brown as a berry from the sun. Tommy Halferty, the drummer from the New Mexicanos. Beats me how he recognised me but, anyway, he tells me he's in the pub business now. Two pubs in Cork and another called The Green Castanets in the Costa Del Sol!'

'You're emigrating,' I said cruelly. I don't think he even heard me.

'The showbands are back in business, he tells me. All the old crew are out of retirement and packing them in in these pubs. He says, "Jimmy boy, get that trumpet out, you were the best." He says, "If it wasn't for the discos you'd be driving this car, Jimmy."'

I couldn't believe what I was hearing and I wasn't impressed – but he wasn't finished yet.

'He says, "Jimmy boy, brass is back, brass is back!" The brass section in the bands, you see, OD. The trombone, the trumpet. See what I'm getting at?'

Mam and me had heard all about comebacks before. The only difference this time was that he was sober when he talked about it. It didn't make it any more real.

'I'm going to give it a shot, OD,' he said. 'I'm buying a trumpet.'

'With what?' I sneered. 'I'm not paying for your pipe dreams. So don't even ask.'

'I wasn't going to,' he answered quietly. 'It's all down to me now, OD.'

I went and washed my cup. He didn't plead for some encouragement like in the old days. He just looked into those ashes. As I left to go to bed, he leaned forward and, picking up the poker, filtered the ashes down through the fire grate.

'Brass is back,' he repeated over and over. 'Brass is back.'

NANCE

The fire brigade had left when Tom and May got home. I'd managed to tidy up the place and our perfect house still looked like it was ready for some photographer to take snaps for one of those glossy 'Homes' magazines. I told them about the chimney fire but not how it started.

'What were you doing, Nance?' was Tom's first reaction. 'The whole place might have gone up!'

May was calmer. Maybe she sensed something in the air beyond the acrid stench of soot. Tom walked around like a headless chicken. For some reason, that limp of his, from some long-ago accident, annoyed me intensely now.

'Are you all right, Nance?' May asked. 'Tom didn't mean . . .'

'Me and my big fires,' he said, trying to hide his embarrassment over his outburst. 'I piled too much coal on before we went out.'

I was shaking. I needed to sit down, but not there and not with them.

'It's just shock,' May said. 'I'll fill a hot water jar for you and …'

'Shock,' I muttered. 'It's shock all right.'

I left them standing there with their worried faces and went up to my bedroom. I locked the door. I got into bed and switched off the light, knowing I wouldn't be able to read as I usually did before I slept. The dark was the same whether my eyes were open or shut. But dark as it was, I could still see the photo. I couldn't figure out what to do next.

All I knew was that I wouldn't be going into school the next day. Even as I was thinking this, I could see I was putting my whole future at risk, just like OD. I found myself blaming him for what I'd done with my books and notes. I couldn't see a way back for myself, and I began to convince myself that I didn't care. All the plans that I'd made – to go to college, become an engineer, see the world – lost their attraction for me.

I didn't want tomorrow to come, but it came anyway. I had to get up early to avoid getting my usual lift into school with Tom.

May did her best to smooth over the ruffles in the sparse conversation, but the sooty stink of the kitchen was like a bad memory. Even if I hadn't yet worked out what I'd do for the day, at least I wasn't shivering any more. May missed the teapot with the water from the kettle but she laughed it off. I pretended not to notice.

'Are you not waiting for a lift?' she asked as I threw on my blazer and grabbed my bag, packed with two old telephone directories and a few ancient *Bunty* and *Judy* annuals I'd dug out from somewhere.

'I feel like walking,' I told her and headed out the back door, pretending not to hear Tom calling from his bedroom window.

Down at Blackcastle Bridge I turned left through the car park and went behind the swimming pool and along the river bank. The bag was heavier than usual so I dumped the annuals in some bushes. The grass on the river's edge was damp so I sat on my bag watching the ducks mess about in their little watery world, nothing to worry them except where the next bite of food was coming from.

I kept telling myself not to look at my watch and I kept looking at it. Nine, quarter past, twenty past, twenty-two minutes past. The breeze along the river was making me shiver again, and I got up and walked for a bit, but the riverside walk came to a sudden stop in a jungle of nettles and I turned back. When I reached my bag I was so frustrated I took aim and kicked it into the water. It went down quicker than I expected and I left it there. I'd just thought of somewhere to hide for a while.

Why I decided to call up to OD's house is a mystery to me. I knew he wouldn't be there, and even if he was I had no intention of talking to him, especially about my book-burning efforts. And Jimmy, though I'd always got on fine with him, wasn't exactly the first one you'd think of bringing your troubles to.

OD had never come out straight with it but I knew he was using the old 'like father, like son' excuse for his own failures. Jimmy was a soft target and I didn't like that. Maybe that was the reason we got on.

Avoiding the Square, where May worked part-time in a health-food shop, I made my way to De Valera Park. OD's house was in the middle of a terrace of eight. It stood out because the neighbouring houses were newly painted and had neat front gardens. Of the three glass panes in OD's front door, the top one was cracked, the second one replaced with plywood and only the bottom one was intact. There was no bell any more. The two wires that used to connect it were twisted upwards like a snake's tongue. On the little unpainted strip where the door knocker used to be, OD had written in a small, tidy hand a Neil Young song title – 'Everybody Knows This Is Nowhere'.

I tapped on the good pane of glass and heard Jimmy shuffling into the hallway. He was having trouble with the door and I waited, wishing I hadn't come, to be sucked into that desolate dump of a house.

If he was surprised to see me, it didn't show. The surprise was all mine. In one hand he held a filthy piece of cloth that used to be a tea towel, in the other was an even filthier nailbrush. Behind him, the post at the end of the stairway was empty of its usual pile of coats. The floor of the hallway had been swept clean of all the dried clay from OD's football boots and all the other dirt that a sweeping brush could shift. There was no clutter of football bags or boots or sweaty gear.

And then I looked at Jimmy's mouth. He had teeth. I'd never seen him with teeth before.

'Well, Nance,' he said, turning red as the words came out in a lispy whistle. 'He's not here, girl.'

I asked him if I could come in, trying to sound casual, trying not to stare at his mouth. It wasn't easy, not when he dabbed the corner of his mouth with that dirty tea towel.

'Sure,' he said and, as if he owed me an explanation, added, 'I was just tidying up a bit.'

When we got to the kitchen I saw what he was at with the nailbrush. The old scarred formica-topped table had been cleared, probably for the first time since his wife left. So far he'd got through about half of it, scrubbing off the sticky bits of gunge. On the dirty half was a pan of brown, sudsy water and beside it – a bar of soap!

I had no right to ask. He was the one who should have been asking questions about my being there, but that wasn't Jimmy's style. I asked anyway.

'What's all this about?'

He hesitated for a moment or two. I could see by the way he was grinding his false teeth that he was in pain and trying hard to overcome it. He cleared off a chair for me and I sat down.

'I'll make some tea,' he said with a twisted smile. 'It's a long story.'

I let myself be carried along on the rising wave of optimism in his words. I was happy for Jimmy. For the first time in years, maybe for the first time ever, he had a plan. The false teeth were only the beginning.

'You can't blow a trumpet without them,' he explained. 'I have to get used to them again. No matter what it takes.'

Then the house. He was going to make it a decent place for them to live in and for people to visit.

'There's no need for all this mess,' he said.

As soon as the house was in order he was going to organise a trumpet for himself. By now, I was so caught up in the whole thing that I was actually forgetting my own troubles, and I decided there and then I was going to help him. I looked around to see if there was any proper cleaning liquid and scrubs under the sink or anywhere else. There was nothing but empty polish tins, rags and an opened packet of washing powder hardened to a slab.

'Have you any money?' I asked.

'Yeah, I'm flush, but I need it for something else.'

'This is a waste of time, Jimmy,' I said, pointing at the nailbrush and the soap. He thought about it.

'How much would all that washing-up gear set me back?'

'You won't have much change from a fiver.'

He went upstairs and was back down, smiling again, sooner than I expected. I noticed how he moved differently, more decisively, and that while he'd been upstairs he'd brushed his long stringy hair back from his forehead and over his ears. That was another first. I'd never seen him with his hair brushed. He had a fiver in his hand. 'Are you sure you have time to do this with me?'

I knew he was asking what on earth I was doing there on a school day. I was writing out a list for him and I didn't look up. I made a start on the place when he'd gone out to the shop and soon found myself taking out all my pent-up feelings on the dirt.

When Jimmy got back we really got down to it. At twelve we broke for tea. Jimmy said the tea had never tasted so good. I nodded in agreement, but it tasted soapy to me.

'Jimmy?' I asked. 'Do you wash the cups with soap too?'

'Yeah, I have the cleanest stomach in Ireland!'

We laughed, but when I think of those words now it makes me feel ill.

By quarter to one we'd transformed the kitchen, the small sitting room and the hall. We'd filled five big black plastic bags with rubbish and the fake lavender smell of air-freshener was, at last, beginning to win the battle with the odour of decay.

I was flattened and Jimmy was hardly able to stand, his knees were so sore from his efforts on the floors. But it only took one look at him, gazing around the place in wonder and disbelief, to feel it had been worthwhile.

25

'Only for you, Nance,' he said, 'I'd still be scrubbing the table.'

In spite of my tiredness, I wanted a few more hours of unthinking labour. I was ready to attack the upstairs bedrooms.

'No way,' he insisted. 'You've done enough. I'll do the rest myself. I just needed someone to show me how to go about it.'

'But I'm not doing anything else today,' I pleaded.

Jimmy looked directly at me and I thought he was going to break the spell of this unexpectedly good morning.

'Why don't you go down and meet OD?' he said. 'He'll be at Super Snax.'

Suddenly, I was close to telling him everything, but then he added, with a fierce but friendly urgency, 'Nance, whatever's bothering you, sort it out quick. Don't let it wait. For God's sake, don't let it wait. This is what happens when you let it wait.'

He was talking about how the house was before we cleaned it up; he was talking about himself.

I went down to Super Snax to find OD and give him one last chance.

OD

On that Monday morning after the St. Peter's match I was wrecked. The thought of going back up to the town park and having another dose of Snipe Doyle would have been awful even without the hangover. Then there was the trouble with my knee.

That must have been the third or fourth week I'd woken up the day after a game and felt those agonising darts of pain. I never felt anything during the game, except that sometimes when I turned too sharply the knee would seem a bit weak and then the sensation would pass. As the weeks went on, I knew I was getting more and more cagey about turning, and I was beginning to wonder if Tom Mahoney noticed.

I guessed it must be cartilage trouble; I should have done something about it but, at the time, football was too important to me. I knew we could win the league and I had to be part of it. Even then, before the storm broke, I was trying to prove that at least in one way I was better than Seanie Moran, that the team needed me more than it needed him.

Seanie was tall for a left winger, and he fancied himself as a cross between Lee Sharpe and Matt Le Tissier. Tricky, so casual he almost seemed lazy, but the laziness was a stunt to put the full back off his guard. The problem for me, at centre forward, was to guess when he was actually going to take on his man and put over the cross.

Off the field he was deadly quiet, but not in the casual way he had when he played. He always seemed to be thinking, worrying and keeping it all to himself. I could never put the two sides of Seanie Moran together. I didn't trust him. He didn't talk to anyone, especially not to me, and I reckoned he thought he was too good for the likes of me, too well-off to be mixing with the son of a down-and-out.

His father, Mick Moran, was a building contractor and developer and hired out heavy machinery. We used his stuff at the park, cement mixers and all that stuff. The Morans had two holidays in the sun every year. Seanie had a permanent tan.

He'd been in my class all through school and a month never went by but some teacher would say, 'Why can't you be like Seanie?' or 'If you worked half as hard as Seanie you'd be top of the class.' I needed that kind of talk like a hole in the head. Football was the only thing I was Number One at, but he was getting better and I knew I was slipping. The worst thing of all was that I depended on him so much. Most of my goals came from his crosses or through-balls. After a goal, we never even shook hands.

Every time I got another dart in the knee I'd think of Seanie, and on that morning Seanie never left my mind. Going downstairs I had to hold on to the banister and in the hallway I limped along by the wall. Jimmy wasn't in the kitchen when I got there, but I couldn't help noticing that the table had been cleared. I'd never realised it was so grotty until then, but I thought nothing of it. My stomach wasn't up to eating so I left for the park before he appeared from wherever he was hiding.

All the way there I was in agony, using the walls and gates along the way as a crutch. Every hundred yards or so I had to stop for a breather – luckily there was no-one around to see me struggle. By the time I reached the park I was managing to get by on my own two feet but I couldn't hide the slight limp like I'd been able to do before. The last person I wanted to be like was Tom Mahoney, but there I was, sharing his trademark limp.

The town park was about three-quarters finished at the time. It was a two-acre site at the edge of town; we'd brought it from a rough field to this in five months. The front area of the site was ready to take the swings and slides for the kids' playground. At the far end from the road we'd planted trees, to enclose an area for people to sit on the stone benches we'd lugged in and cemented together. In the centre of this area we'd built a huge rockery around a fountain which was a statue of a fish spitting into about four feet of water.

To the left and right of the rockery were two patches of grass with the borders dug out for flowers. Around the fountain and the grass we were laying a pebble path for people to dawdle along – the old folk, the mothers with their prams, the unemployed with nothing better to do. Sometimes I wondered if I'd end up spending my days sitting there or walking around in circles. Looking at a stone fish.

The first person I saw that morning was Beano. He looked worried. Which is hardly news. As I came in by the gate, he pointed to the cabin, over at the right side of the park, from which Snipe kept a watch on us. I should have had the sense to walk around by the back of that prefab unit, but I didn't feel like sneaking about like a frightened slave. So I hobbled past the open door.

Snipe didn't notice me at first – stuck into the racing pages of *The Sun*, more than likely – and I thought I'd gotten away with being a half hour late. Before I got to Beano's side, I heard Snipe yelp, 'Ryan!'

I ignored him and grabbed a shovel. He stuck his round little face out the window of the cabin.

'Over here, you chancer. Now!'

Beano took the shovel from me and started to pile some pebbles into a wheelbarrow.

'Go on, OD,' he whispered. 'His bite is worse than his bark.'

'Not funny, Beano.'

'Please,' he said. I knew he meant that if Snipe lost his rag he wouldn't only take it out on me but on Beano too.

I remembered how Beano had saved me the embarrassment of turning up at Nance's at one in the morning. For his sake, I limped over to the cabin. As I came in, Snipe shoved his newspaper under a folder of plans for the site.

'Well?' I asked, looking at the desk where a corner of *The Sun* was sticking out. 'Any developments in the political situation?'

He cut me with a look.

'Or the Michael Jackson story? Is it true he's having a baby?'

I don't think he even got that one.

'You're half an hour late – again.' My knee was reminding me of its pain. I was having trouble standing so I sat on the edge of his desk.

'Get your rear end off my plans.'

'I can't stand,' I said. 'I hurt my leg in the match yesterday.'

He fixed his rugby-club tie, his touchstone of respectability. He fingered it like it was sacred.

'A soccer player!' he said. 'You wouldn't last five minutes in a real game. I'm docking you, Ryan. Now get out there and do something.'

He'd threatened to dock me before but never gone through with it. I wasn't worried. The crack about the rugby bugged me more – which only proves how scattered my head was, to let something stupid like that get to me. Still, I was able to stay calm. I lifted myself from the desk and breezed out the door – holding it all in; a million miles, I thought, from breaking point.

Naturally enough, me and Beano had a rough morning after that. I didn't mind too much since I was the centre of attention because of my goal against St. Peter's. Just the same, when it got to lunchtime, I was sore all over from the lifting and dragging and trying to keep the weight off my knee.

I wasn't in the best of form for meeting Nance. Too much caught up in my own misery, I wasn't up to appreciating hers. Last night's tiff was just that, a tiff, the kind of thing we'd got over before. It didn't even occur to me to wonder why Nance came into Super Snax. Usually we met after I'd finished there and she'd be back from her own house or from the shop May worked in.

Beano stood up when she came in. He always did that. I never got around to asking him where he picked that up. Probably from a Jack Nicholson film. He was a Nicholson addict, throwing in lines from his films every so often and usually getting them slightly or badly wrong. He made an excuse about having to go somewhere and went. I wished he'd stayed. I mightn't have been so unpleasant with Nance if he had. If 'if's were pounds, I'd be a millionaire.

'Have a chip,' I said without looking up from my plate, feeling sorry for myself. She sat opposite but didn't speak for a bit. When I glanced up at her she was looking away. At the same time as I was thinking how beautiful she was, the back of my knee felt like someone was sticking an ice-pick in it. I must have groaned or let out a sharp sigh or something because she looked at me suddenly with her big brown eyes. For a split second it was like she was staring at a stranger.

'Are you all right?' she asked.

I told her about the knee and about my wonderful morning at the park. She didn't react as I'd wanted her to. There was no sympathy. She didn't even get mad and tell me she was tired of listening to my complaints, though I guessed she was.

'What about you?' I asked trying to disguise my disappointment.

'Me?'

'Yeah, what kind of morning did you have?'

After a moment she told me about her morning as a charlady for Jimmy. I freaked. I didn't think of asking her why she'd skipped school, I was so mad.

'You had no right to be poking around up there,' I told her. 'He had a skivvy for eighteen years and he never thanked her for it.'

Then she stuck the knife in.

'Did you thank her?'

I couldn't get an answer out and I was afraid I was going to lose it. Then she softened.

'Don't you want Jimmy to make a new start?'

'I'm up to here with Jimmy's new starts.'

'And I'm up to here with you, OD.'

I threw my fork onto the plate. It hit the tomato sauce and sprayed the front of her school blouse with red droplets. She didn't seem to care. She stood up and gave me one last look, as if she was waiting for me to say something. I wanted to apologise but all I could think of was Jimmy. If he could say he was making a comeback, why couldn't I? That was what all this was about, I thought, wasn't it? I said nothing. When she reached the door and had pushed it out, she called back over her shoulder, 'You'd never think of asking why, would you?'

But I was still thinking about Jimmy up at De Valera Park, not about Nance. She was already out of sight when I shouted at the swinging door, 'Cause he's a dumb dreamer, is why!'

I pushed away the plate and told myself we'd make up later, when we'd calmed down. What's a few harsh words between friends, I thought. Like a fool.

NANCE

It was going to be a long afternoon and it was getting colder. I could have gone home and waited. I could have gone up to Jimmy's again. Instead I went back down to the river. There was no plan in my head, just Jimmy's ringing words – 'don't let it wait'.

I drifted along the same stretch I'd been on earlier, until I found the spot of flattened grass where I'd been sitting. This time I didn't care about the damp. If I got a cold out of sitting there, I'd have something else to hide behind.

After a while, I broke off a long branch from a tree over-hanging the water and began fishing absent-mindedly for my bag. I was surprised at how quickly I found it. Raising it up on the stick, I held it away from me so the water would pour out. Then I opened it and lifted out the sodden telephone directories.

There was an '05' and an '06'. The '06', I knew, covered parts of Tipperary, Clare … and Limerick. Heather Kelly from Limerick. My natural mother.

I went through the soggy pages as carefully as I could, but they kept coming away in my hand. Eventually, I found the Kellys. Two pages of them. I counted the '061's for Limerick. Two hundred and sixteen! I ditched the phone book back in the water.

'Don't let it wait,' I heard Jimmy say over and over. The notion of finding Heather Kelly took hold of me. Crazy ideas went in and out of my head. Hiring a private detective, putting an ad in the *Limerick Leader*. In the end, I got nowhere but I felt calmer. Somehow, I felt that now I'd decided to search for Heather, a way would reveal itself. One thing I was sure of: Tom and May would know nothing about my search, not if I could help it. I didn't hate them. I wasn't sure any more how I felt about them. It was after four by now, and from where I sat I could see the crowd from our school going home. Time to face the music.

They were both waiting for me when I got in. May was quiet but kept staring at me; for a mad instant, I imagined she'd figured out what was wrong. I even imagined that look she gave me was one of understanding, until it became clear that it was just plain incomprehension written all over her face.

I had always been the perfect daughter of a perfect family. We were comfortably off. A nice detached house in the best part of town; a good car but not a flash one; summer holidays in Spain, Portugal, France. Tom and May never wasted time on anything that wasn't useful. And I played my own part to perfection. I was good at school, at games, I stayed out of trouble – even when I was with OD. Apart from the usual rows that all families have from time to time, there had never been any real conflict between the three of us. Not until now.

Tom was holding nothing back. He sounded like he was more concerned with his own reputation than anything else.

'The bloody embarrassment of it,' he raged, 'making excuses for you all day and no idea where you were. What the hell are you up to?'

I wasn't going to tell him any lies. Lies, other people's lies, were at the bottom of all my troubles. So I said nothing at all.

'Why?' May asked in a whisper. I almost said, 'Why what?' but I kept my silence.

Tom was losing patience. He looked at the shelf where I usually threw my bag when I came in.

'Where's your schoolbag?'

'It's gone,' I said evenly.

'Gone?' May said.

They both sat down at the kitchen table and I was left standing before them. It was like the principal's office at school, or how I imagined it might be if you were in trouble. Not that I, being so perfect, ever was.

'What did you do with it?' he wanted to know, but his voice had none of the authority you'd expect in a principal's office.

'I threw it in the river.'

'Sit down, Nance,' May said. 'Tell us what's wrong.'

I tried to resist her pleading eyes but I couldn't. Tom was shaking his head in disbelief. He didn't seem able to lift his eyes.

'And your books? The whole lot? In the river?' he was asking the table.

'No.'

They looked at each other and May picked up the question he was afraid to ask.

'I burned them all last night,' I told her. 'That's what started the chimney fire. I'm sorry about the fire.'

'What is it all about?' Tom asked. 'It's something to do with OD, isn't it?'

May took his hand, trying to change his line of attack. He pulled away from her and went on.

'I warned you about him, Nance,' he said. 'He's bad news, always was, always will … '

I let him rant on because nothing he could say frightened me more than seeing him draw away from May like that. I wondered if my search for the truth would drive them apart even further, and the temptation to tell them I'd found the photo was growing. If he hadn't kept going on about OD I might have given in.

'You had a row with him, I suppose,' he said, 'and now it's the end of the world. For God's sake, Nance, I thought you'd have more cop-on than that.'

Then I surprised myself. I said something I hadn't

planned to say. As soon as I did I knew it was true.

'I'm not going out with OD any more,' I told Tom. 'This has nothing to do with him.'

'Since when?' he asked suspiciously.

'I didn't burn my books because of OD,' I said. 'I went mental and I can't explain why ... I don't know why.'

May came around to my side of the table. Her arm was over my shoulder. It took a huge effort not to pull away as Tom had done.

'Is it the exams?' she asked. 'Don't think we'll judge you by how many honours you get, Nance. We just want you to be happy.'

I didn't answer. By now, I was playing for sympathy, my best chance of escape from this unpleasantness. Tom was thinking hard. I suppose it was his way of dealing with things: thinking about the practicalities of getting me back on the rails, the school-rails.

'I'll sort out the books,' he said. 'Did you burn your copies and notes too?'

I nodded.

'We'll work something out,' he told May. 'I'll tell them I was tidying out the place, after the chimney fire or something, and dumped Nance's stuff by acc–'

'I'm not going back,' I said.

'In a few days,' May said hopefully. 'You need a break from studying.'

I released myself from her hold and got to the door. When

I looked back at them I saw them as if they were in a photograph, could almost see the jagged-edged fold like a shaft of lightning between them. In a few days maybe I'll go back, I thought. If I find Heather Kelly. But not before.

And, I thought, this is not my fault. This is your own doing, the two of you. I'm not your little black baby any more. I'm the daughter of Heather Kelly and a man whose name I don't know. I belong to a different race or in some limbo between two races.

In my room, I found a biro and an old notepad. The little cuddly bear with the glowing heart on the head of the paper seemed to be laughing at me for believing in innocent love. Dear OD, I began, wondering if the three pages left in the notepad gave me enough space to put down everything I felt. A quarter of a page was enough. When you leave out the real reasons and the passing of blame and the pain of being let down, there's not much to say in a goodbye letter.

I found a coat and went up to Beano's house, at the far end of De Valera Park from OD's. I asked Beano to give the letter to OD. He smiled his mad smile, but he knew better than most of us what was going on in the real world. I was sure he had no doubt about what was in the letter.

'The park'll be finished in a month,' he said. 'OD won't hang around waiting for the next scheme. I bet he'll go back to school.'

'I don't think so, Beano.'

'But he might, if …'

If I was still around to persuade him, he meant. He still hadn't pocketed the letter; he was holding it out so that I could have taken it back if I'd wanted to.

'Give it to him as soon as you can,' I said and turned to go.

'Right,' he said. 'I'll be meeting him at half six ...'

I kept on walking.

'At the snooker hall,' Beano called after me.

And I kept on walking.

OD

Beano and me were the last ones to leave the site that evening. We'd been given the job of locking away all the shovels and wheelbarrows and stuff, because Snipe was off early to the bookies. We were locking the main gate when Mick Moran drove up in his new silver Range Rover. Seanie was in the passenger seat.

Mick Moran was a big thick-set fellow with tight sandy hair cropped close to his head. On the coldest of days he wore a shirt with the sleeves rolled up and the buttons open halfway down his hairy chest. He was so busy making money he didn't notice the weather. The window of the Range Rover slid down.

'Hard at it, lads,' he said. 'Is Mr. Doyle around?'

'No,' I muttered, concentrating on holding the gate for Beano to fix the lock on.

Beano's hand was shaking too much to fit the key. People like Moran made him nervous. Which was bad news for

Beano, because the world is full of Mick Morans.

'He's … he's down with the Town Clerk … at the Council Offices,' he said, with all the certainty of a bad liar.

I let out a snigger and Moran gave me one of his hard-man looks. He got out of the Range Rover and came over to Beano.

'You wouldn't mind opening the cabin for me, young lad, would you?' he asked pleasantly. 'I need to check something there.'

'We're closing up,' I told him. 'You can talk to Mr. Doyle at the Council Offices.' Moran looked me up and down like I was a particularly awkward tree stump in the path of one of his JCBs.

'I'm in a hurry,' he said and slid back the handle of the gate. 'I won't keep ye long.'

Beano followed him into the site and I was left standing there staring at Seanie, who was stuck in one of his schoolbooks. I'm sure he must have felt my eyes burning into him, because he seemed to be stuck on the same page for a long time. Then he looked up at me.

'How's it going?' he said.

'Could be worse.'

'How's the knee?'

I felt a twinge and my stomach was suddenly empty, or full of something that shouldn't have been there. I moved towards the Range Rover.

'There's nothing wrong with my knee,' I said.

43

'I just thought … the way you were turning yesterday … it wasn't …'

'My knee's perfect, Moran. And don't go mouthing off to Mahoney about it.'

Which was not very clever. If my knee was really all right then it wouldn't matter what he said to Mahoney. Besides, I'd never known him to speak to Mahoney except to answer a question.

Mick Moran and Beano were on their way back. I felt so stupid I had to offer an explanation.

'You know how it is with me and Mahoney,' I said. 'He's only waiting for the chance to drop me.'

'Because of Nance?'

I didn't like the sound of Nance's name on Seanie's lips. 'Listen, Seanie,' I said, 'keep your nose where it belongs – stuck in your books.'

I felt Mick Moran's hand on my back and I dropped my shoulder to shrug it off. He looked from me to Seanie.

'Is he getting at you, Seanie?' he asked, doing the old Clint Eastwood grinding of the jaw.

'No.'

''Cause if he is, I'll go through him for a short cut.' Seanie didn't look happy. He started to answer but changed his mind and turned away. Mick Moran squared up to me.

'Do you have a problem, son?' he demanded.

'I wouldn't call it a problem,' I said. 'I just don't like you, Moran.'

He snapped his fist out towards me but I didn't flinch. He held my shoulder in a grip that looked friendly but felt like a vice.

'Son,' he said, 'the feeling is mutual.'

He let go and piled heavily in behind the steering wheel. Beano had dropped the lock and was on his knees searching for the bundle of keys. Moran pulled away in the Range Rover.

'He'll kill me,' Beano was moaning, but I wasn't listening.

My eyes were fixed on Moran's, which were glaring at me from the side mirror. I gave him the finger and the brakes screeched. I could see Seanie spin round to his old man, and after a few seconds they moved away again. Moran's hand came into view. He was returning my message.

When I turned around, Beano was fumbling with the gate again. I grabbed the keys from him and Beano laughed in his hurt, defensive way.

'You'll get yourself creased one of these days, OD!'

'Not before I crease someone else,' I said. 'What was he at in there?'

'Looking at the plans or something. I don't know.'

On the way home I kept thinking of Nance. From the minute Seanie had mentioned her name I had known I should go and talk to her, tell her I was sorry for getting thick. I planned on getting changed quickly and heading over to her place straight away. It didn't work out like that.

As soon as I opened the front door, the smell of air-

45

freshener hit me. Then I saw the hallway, tiles spick and span, nothing left around to clog up the place. The kitchen was spotless too, and in the fireplace no ashes sagged out from beneath the grate. Instead a few briquettes were formed neatly into a pyramid. At the base of this pyramid, like a garland of flowers, lay an assortment of crumpled-up strips of toilet paper. Each one was stained with blood. I heard Jimmy's footsteps moving back and forth in his bedroom directly above. I went slowly up the stairs, afraid of what I was going to find. It couldn't have been a shaving cut. There were too many of those blood-stained tissues for that.

His bedroom door was open. He was standing on a chair beside the wardrobe. In his hand was the wide-brimmed sombrero from his showband days. I couldn't see any blood on him.

He hadn't heard me come in and he tottered on the chair when he saw me. I rushed in and steadied him. The sombrero slipped sideways in his hand and I saw, but pretended not to, a crisp tenner inside it.

'What are you doing?' I yelled. 'You'll break your neck off that chair.'

He placed the sombrero carefully on top of the wardrobe and I helped him down. I hated touching him. I could feel his sweat on the purple nylon shirt he wore.

'Some job,' he said. 'What do you think?'

How long is this 'comeback' going to last? was what I was thinking. Until the next binge? Until the latest pipe-dream comes crashing down around your ears?

'Why did you let Nance do all this?' I shouted. 'D'ye think all women are skivvies?'

He flicked the long hair back behind his ears. It was a habit that really bugged me; it was the kind of thing a young fellow did, not a decrepit, middle-aged has-been.

'I didn't ask her to do it,' he said and took a piece of toilet paper from his pocket to wipe his mouth.

I saw the smudge of pink on the tissue before I noticed the teeth.

'I'm giving the old teeth another shot,' he said. 'So I can blow the trumpet, you know.'

I didn't really mean to laugh at him. It was a mixture of relief and pity that made me do it. Relief that the bloody tissues had been explained; pity at the pain in his raw gums. Of course, it didn't come out like that. He turned away and went back to filling a black plastic bag with old shoes and empty cigarette packets – and the old *Spotlight* magazines with their pictures of him as a young man. I nearly asked him not to throw them out, but I felt so miserable about breaking up in front of him that I retreated to the kitchen.

I sat watching the telly but I didn't turn up the sound. There was a music video on. A woman walked in slow motion away from the camera through a field of long grass. I wondered where Mam was now. London, Jimmy had told me the day after she left, but we had no address. She hadn't written. When I asked if she'd left a note, I knew by his unconvincing denial that she had. Not that it mattered. I wouldn't have been able to bring myself to read it anyway.

Every so often the picture on the telly would start to roll, as it had been doing for months. I'd never got around to fixing it though I was good at that kind of thing – electrics, machines. I just couldn't be bothered fixing anything in that house. It seemed to me that everything was meant to stay broken there.

After a few minutes, Jimmy arrived in the kitchen with the big plastic bag and lugged it out by the back door. Outside, he stacked it alongside five or six others. Back inside, he put on the kettle and waited for it to boil.

'Did you throw out any of my gear?' I asked, spoiling for an argument.

'It's all in a bag under the stairs,' he said. 'You can sort it out yourself.'

'Were you messing around in my room too?'

'No.'

The Angelus came on the telly with a picture of a Navajo mother and child. I'd arranged to meet Beano at the snooker hall at half six, thinking I'd have cleared the air with Nance by then. That would take more than half an hour, so I decided to call up to her after I'd had my game of snooker.

Jimmy laid out the one good set of cups and saucers for the tea – which tasted a little better than usual and looked the right colour for a change. He wasn't eating anything, and the click of his false teeth against the rim of the cup was the only sound in the kitchen apart from the low buzz of the telly.

The sense of calm radiating from him amazed me. I knew he must be in agony but it was like he was in some dreamland, some Graceland of the soul, where pain didn't matter. He was far away, but not as far away as I supposed. Out of the blue, he said, 'Why wasn't Nance in school today? Did she tell you?'

Too embarrassed to say I hadn't even thought of asking, I shook my head. It wasn't very pleasant to be faced with my own blind stupidity. To have it pointed out to me by a high-plains drifter like Jimmy was even worse.

I let down my cup too sharply on its saucer and a little chip came off the base. Sorry, I said to myself. Sorry, Nance. At the same time I was answering myself. Too late now, OD, too bloody late for 'sorry' now.

NANCE

It didn't seem like a coincidence to me when Seanie Moran came to our house that evening for a 'grind' from Tom. When I heard the doorbell ringing I was certain it was OD, and I thought I'd better get to the door before he and Tom confronted each other. OD was sure to blame him for our break-up.

The frosty look I had prepared for OD unnerved Seanie as he stood in the open doorway. He shuffled his books from one hand to the other.

'Is your father around?' he asked. 'I'm taking economic history as an extra subject. Tom … Mr. Mahoney is going to help me out.'

I wasn't making a move; my mind was on that young Kenyan in the photo, wondering what he looked like now that he had been rescued in my mind from that car crash. Seanie was getting uneasy. He kept looking past me, hoping Tom would appear. 'He said half past six. Maybe he forgot.'

'No, he's here,' I said, at last. 'I'll get him. Come in.'

I brought him into the study and went to fetch Tom. He was in the bath.

'Five minutes,' he called, over the noise of the radio he always brought in there with him.

Downstairs again, I went to the study door and told Seanie.

'Are you all right?' he asked. 'I mean … you weren't in school today. I thought maybe you were sick or something.'

That he should have noticed I was out was surprising enough, but his breaking of the rule of silence he kept towards everyone in the class was even more so. Most of the fellows in our year didn't like Seanie, but there were a few girls who harboured not-so-secret longings for him. Like OD, I was inclined to believe he was a bit of a snob and maybe a bit weird too.

'I'm fine,' I said, still holding on to the door handle.

'You didn't miss anything much,' he said. Then racking his brain for something else to say, he added, 'You'll be back tomorrow so, I suppose.'

For a moment I wondered if it was possible that the word was already out about my breaking up with OD and whether Seanie was making a ham-fisted play for me. Then I got suspicious. It seemed strange that Tom hadn't mentioned anything during the last few days about giving Seanie a grind. Besides, Tom never gave grinds. He was always too busy.

I sat down close to Seanie, but not too close, to have a

good look at the textbook in his hand. It wasn't familiar. Maybe he really was doing economic history. But why? He wasn't likely to be scraping for points and economic history had nothing to do with medicine, which we all knew he was aiming for. He was big into the Red Cross and was already an instructor on their First Aid courses.

'Why would a doctor want to know about economic history?' I asked casually.

I thought he was going to clam up then, because he suddenly looked so unhappy. When he spoke, his tone was dead flat.

'I've changed my mind about medicine,' he shrugged, 'I'm trying for accountancy.'

'That's a bit drastic,' I said, 'from medicine to accountancy?'

'Dad's business is getting bigger,' he explained. 'He's branching out into all kinds of things and he reckons I'll need to be an accountant to handle it.'

'So it's his idea?'

'No,' Seanie insisted. 'Anyway, he built the business up for me. I can't just walk away from it, can I?'

It sounded more like a plea than a question. He seemed to want to tell me more but I felt I'd poked my nose in far enough already. I changed the subject.

'And I thought you were here to talk me into going back to school,' I said. Then he turned the tables on me. 'You weren't sick today, were you, Nance?'

'No,' I said.

'If there's anything I can do …' he began uncertainly, 'I'd like to help you.'

'I don't need any help.'

'What I mean is, if it helped for you to talk about it, I'd be glad to listen,' he said. 'I'm not saying I can sort anything out for you but …'

We could hear Tom coming down the stairs. I stood up and Seanie stared miserably at his economic history book, sorry he'd said anything.

At the door I almost bumped into Tom. I circled around him like he had the plague and the smile on his face sagged. He closed the door of the study with a bang and I went away to my bedroom.

I thought about Seanie and how he'd opened up so unexpectedly; how, unlike OD, he'd sensed I was in some kind of trouble. I thought about my reasons for disliking him and realised they were all second-hand – and came from OD. How many more of my opinions, I wondered, were really OD's? Even the notion of leaving school was a copycat one – even if, for the moment, I couldn't see an alternative. Now that I'd broken off with OD, I'd have to think for myself. That couldn't be bad. The thought made me feel better.

In the sitting room downstairs, I found May doing one of her water-colours at the long oval table. The smell of the paint reminded me of better times, when there were no big complications in my life and I could marvel at her talent for getting a tree or a sky just right. Now, I didn't even bother to look at her picture. I switched on the telly to watch *Home and Away*, knowing she didn't approve and willing her, for once, to say so. Tom was never slow to.

As she dabbed away carefully with her brushes I sneaked sideways glances at her. With her jet-black hair and olive skin she looked more Italian or Spanish than Irish. I realised what a strange threesome we made, posing as the ideal family. Tom, the perfect caricature of a redheaded, brown-eyed Irishman; his Mediterranean wife; his daughter, darker still.

What, I wondered, did people make of us? Did they make jokes or swap snide, sarcastic comments? Because I'd never bothered about what people thought of me before, these questions – the very fact that they came up – were a terrible shock to my system. I felt like my whole world was narrowing down and I was becoming more and more isolated – an alien within an alien family.

I realised, too, that my isolation had begun long before I found the photo. In fact, it had begun around the time I took up with OD. Up to then I had two really close friends: Siobhan Dudley and Kelly Esmonde. Of the two, I was closest to Siobhan who was a year older than me and was now in Edinburgh University. That wouldn't have been so bad, but her parents had moved to Scotland too when her father got a new job over there.

Kelly Esmonde was a classmate. From the start she warned me about OD, and OD must have known because he worked hard on turning me against her. I let the friendship slip away. I suppose I thought that having OD was enough. It wasn't. Now I had no one, and trying to make up with Kelly would have been like admitting defeat. The truth was that the nearest thing to a friend I'd had since I met OD was May. But that only made the big deception even harder to take. Just as I was telling myself that this was my chance to talk, it occurred to me that it was her chance too and that she wasn't even trying – so why should I?

Outside in the hallway, Tom was seeing Seanie to the door. Their lowered voices made me feel paranoid. When he came into the room I turned up the volume on the remote.

'What was all that in aid of?' he asked.

'All what?' May said, looking up from her work.

He stepped around my chair and stood between me and *Home and Away.*

'Nance,' he demanded, 'why did you do that to me? In front of young Moran!'

'I did nothing.'

'You walked around me as if I was some kind of child-beater.'

May put down her paintbrush and came over to take the remote from the arm of my chair. She switched off the telly and sat on the chair next to mine.

'We have to talk, Nance,' she said. 'Tell us what's on your mind … please.'

I was watching Tom and I could see he was near to cracking. I wanted to push him over the edge.

'Why did you bring Seanie Moran up here this evening?'

He looked at May in confusion. She was lost too. Or else they were acting well.

'He was supposed to get around me about going back, wasn't he?' I said, even though I didn't believe that any more – it was just a stick to beat him with.

Easing himself back into a chair, he looked at me like he was having trouble focusing his eyes.

'What kind of father do you think I am?' he said. 'Is this all I get for …' I got to my feet quickly.

'For what?' I cried. 'For saving a black baby from the jungle?'

May tried to touch me but I wouldn't let her.

'I'm not a baby any more,' I told them both. Something about them keeping me in the dark almost slipped out, but I held my tongue.

'Is it one of the staff?' Tom asked desperately. 'Or one of the other kids?'

'I'm not a kid.'

'We can't talk sense,' May said, 'if you won't tell us the truth.'

'Exactly!' I said.

I don't know if you can really feel these things in the air or whether you just imagine you do, but I'm sure I felt the sinking in their stomachs. The very room seemed to be sinking. I rushed to the door, knowing I had to escape before we all went down together.

OD

It was a quarter to seven. Beano was late and I'd already started a game with Pat Doran. 'Rowdy', we called him, because he was so quiet. He was the only person I knew who apologised before he made a mistake.

I was on a roll. The reds were dropping in fast and the set-up for the black was coming right every time. I was lining up the black again and ready to move on to the colours. Concentrating hard, as much to forget my troubles as to hit a good shot, I bent down low over the cue. Just as I drew back the cue the door burst open.

'Honey, I'm back!' Beano yelped, a mad leer on his face.

That was supposed to be Jack Nicholson in *The Shining*. The tip of my cue went into the green baize and puckered it. I threw down the cue and made for him. He nipped around to the other side of the table, and for a while we dodged around it like two cartoon characters. I almost had him when he produced the letter and held it out to me.

'Nance asked me to give you this,' he said. My stomach hit the floor.

Rowdy waited quietly for the game to continue, but I wasn't interested. He pretended to be busy chalking his cue. I went over and sat in the corner and got myself psyched up to open the envelope.

'Finish the game for me, Beano,' I said.

'Right! Who's on? Me? Right.'

'You're on the black,' Rowdy whispered.

The paper was ridiculously childish, but the writing was firm and the contents far from innocent.

Dear OD,

We don't belong together. I'm not sure if we ever did. We both need to sort ourselves out and since we can't help each other to do that, there's no point in carrying on. Don't try to change my mind, it would only make things worse.

Nance.

I kept re-reading it as if, by some miracle, some more lines would appear and explain why she'd come to this conclusion now. We both knew what I had to sort out, but what was her problem? The mitching from school had something to do with it and, now that I thought about it, she'd been in a strange humour for the past few weeks. Was she getting panicky over the exams and maybe thinking she couldn't afford to waste any more time with me? Or had Tom finally got to her and convinced her I was no good for her?

I fixed my rage on Tom. I imagined facing up to him and explaining with my fists what I thought of him. I'd pull out of the Youths team and he'd soon see he couldn't do without me. Which would be playing right into his hands. I shelved that idea.

The last line of the letter seemed to cut off any hope of getting to her. That and my stupid pride. I wouldn't crawl back, not to anyone. Well, so I thought.

Beano had finished the game, managing to get beaten though I was well ahead when I handed over. He came over to me and sprawled himself out on the long bench where I was holed up in the corner.

'That table is lop-sided,' he declared. 'And the cushions are dead.'

I rolled the letter into a ball and shoved it in my pocket. I got myself up from the bench and my knee felt stiff from sitting.

'We're going for a pint,' I said.

'It's a bit early, OD,' Beano objected.

'Right,' I told him as I headed for the door, 'I'm going for a pint.'

He followed me out into Friary Street and had trouble keeping up, I was in such a hurry. When we got to the door of the Galtee Lounge, part of me, the thing the nuns used to tell me in primary school was my guardian angel, was saying, 'Don't go in.'

I went ahead.

We talked about football all night, going through the endless permutations of what might happen in the League. What if St. Peter's beat Evergreen Celtic the following Saturday and we lost to Cashel? And what if we dropped a point and St. Peter's went on winning and it came down to the last game where a draw would do for them but only a win would be good enough for us? It was all comfortable nonsense, and it would have been fine if I'd left it at that.

I was drinking too quickly and with every pint the Coke in Beano's glass annoyed me more. Beano never drank alcohol and I'd never pushed him to. Until that night. That night I felt like I was drifting away on a slow boat to nowhere and he was on the shore, sober and leaving me to drown alone.

'Have a drink,' I insisted. 'Just the one,'

'I have a drink.'

'That's not a drink. It's coloured water.'

Then I started grovelling, searching for pity and companionship on my boat. 'Beano,' I pleaded, 'you know what's after happening between me and Nance. I'm on my own now.'

'I'm here, aren't I?' Beano said, but I could see I was getting through.

'It's not the same. I might as well be drinking with … with …' I was trying to think of someone else who didn't drink, 'with … Doctor Seanie Moran.'

'Will we play a game of pool?' Beano tried.

'You're avoiding the question.'

'You didn't ask me a question,' Beano said innocently.

'The question is, are you having a pint or are you going to get lost?'

He had two pints. I never thought an albino could get any paler but, as we left the Galtee Lounge, Beano was the colour of death. He was even more unsteady on his feet than I was and the closer we got to De Valera Park, the quieter he got. In a way it was like old times. I was back to taking care of him like when he was younger.

When we reached the gate of his house, he didn't want to go in. He said he wanted to walk some more, but my knee was bothering me again and I needed to lie down so my head would stop spinning. He kept on insisting until I got fed up of it and went home, leaving him standing at the gate like a dead man at the door of Heaven – or Hell.

The streetlight near our house was on the blink again and I had trouble getting the key in the door. Inside, the silence was so complete I went instinctively to Jimmy's room. When I looked in on him, I heard a sudden contented snore as if all was right in his dream world.

As my eyes got used to the dark, I noticed a half-empty glass on his bedside table. I picked up the glass and took a whiff, but it was just water. Which was just as well for him. If it had been whiskey I'd have poured it over his head. I stumbled away in the dark to my bed.

The sleep I hoped for didn't come. My mind searched

through the debris of the last few weeks with Nance and picked up the traces of trouble that should have been obvious to me all along. Of course, I only made a kind of drunken sense of them.

Nance, I decided, had been preparing me for the worst. She was withdrawn, not because of some passing mood, but because she was loosening the ties between us. There could be only one reason for that. Not the exams and, I decided, not Tom either. There was someone else involved, another fellow. And if that was the case I wasn't going to get into a sweat over it. I was bigger than all that mush. Like I said before, there was no one I would crawl after. Now I had a reason. There was no one who would crawl after me.

NANCE

Over the next few days I saw a lot of Seanie Moran. Tom was anxious to get through the course with him as quickly as possible so he could concentrate on his own classes. After that first evening Seanie never mentioned school or asked when – or if – I was going back.

It became a nightly ritual. I'd answer the door, take him into the study, talk for a while; later, when they'd finished, I always happened to be around to see him out. We'd talk again and the doorstep conversation went from five minutes the first night to maybe ten the following evening, until by Saturday night of that week we were talking for a good hour.

He was my only contact with the outside world by this time. Tom and May had backed off altogether and, though it was confusing, it was a relief too. With OD gone from the picture, it was hardly surprising that I finally began to drop hints about my problem to Seanie that evening.

I already knew from the look on Tom's face when he'd

come in earlier that his team had been beaten by Cashel. If it had been OD on the doorstep we would have been talking football and nothing else. Seanie just mentioned it in passing, adding that he'd had a lousy game.

I brought him around to his decision about medicine again. I'd been building up gradually to this all week. If I could fool myself that I was helping him then it would be easier to accept his help.

'Are you giving up the Red Cross too?' I asked.

Seanie wasn't pleased with the direction of the conversation.

'I don't have time for all that now,' he said.

'I think you're crazy, trying to please your father instead of doing what you really want to do.'

'So what do I do? "Thanks, Dad, but no thanks for twenty-five years of hard labour"?'

'Do you really think he did it all for you?'

'Maybe not, but that's how he sees it,' he said weakly.

I suddenly found myself back in the thick of my own difficulties again. When I asked if Mick Moran had really done it all for Seanie, I immediately thought of Tom and May. Had they done it all for me or just to fill a gap in their own lives? The idea left me feeling used.

Out of nowhere, before I even knew I was going to do it, I found myself saying Heather Kelly's name.

'I have to find a woman called Heather Kelly. That's the only way I can go back to school.'

Seanie's next question was inevitable. I'd trapped him into it.

'Who's Heather Kelly?'

Just then, Johnny Regan, the creep I'd given the Guinness shampoo to, passed by the gate. He gave me the usual dirty look, but it quickly changed to a sinister smile. Seanie took one look at Johnny and winced. I felt I had to keep talking before he backed off.

'She worked with Tom and May in Kenya. I want to meet her.'

'Wouldn't they tell you where she is?'

'I'd prefer if they didn't know I was looking for her,' I said.

Something seemed to click in his mind because his eyes narrowed and then widened again.

'I don't know why you want to find this woman. It's none of my business, but I might be able to help.'

The clouds of those last few days seemed to part for an instant. I was quaking inside, full of expectation – and terror.

'Last year,' he explained, 'I entered this essay competition about Third World Development and I asked Tom for some ideas. He put me in touch with this priest, Father O'Brien, who was in Kenya with him. He was very old and I don't think he was very well. Maybe he's … you know, maybe he's not around any more.'

I refused to consider the possibility that the priest was dead.

'Will you ask him for me?'

'Sure,' he said. 'He's in Dublin but I still have his phone number.'

I knew he wanted me to tell him more, but I was afraid that if I did he'd have second thoughts about it.

'What's the story with OD?' he asked me. 'Are you still with him?'

I shook my head and, stepping back, eased the door inwards.

'It's just that …' he began, but I cut him off.

'Seanie, it's not a good time to … talk about that stuff.'

'You're picking me up all wrong, Nance,' he said. There was a deep blush beneath his tanned skin. 'Look, I'll ring you as soon as I talk to him, all right? And Nance?'

'Yeah?'

'I'm not … I'm not looking for anything, OK?'

Even though he'd proved himself a nice fellow, I didn't believe him. But I smiled gratefully and went inside.

As I passed through the hallway I caught a glimpse of Tom through the open door of the study. He looked shattered as he stared out over his PC in the direction of the mantelpiece. Maybe I was wrong, but I thought I knew what he was staring at. A 'family' photo, taken on my confirmation day. All those long-ago smiles seemed to me like a pretence, where only the child was really fooled. And the child in me was gone.

May was in the kitchen making some of the necklaces and

earrings she sold, along with her water-colours, as a sideline at the health food shop. I searched through the fridge and the kitchen presses, not looking for anything in particular. I wanted to stay in the kitchen and be near her but I wasn't sure why. I poured some muesli into a bowl.

'We've been talking, Nance,' May said and I waited for her 'softly, softly' approach at persuading me to begin again.

'Tom feels that he may have put too much pressure on you. He wants you to know that he never meant to do that.'

I stirred milk into the muesli and spooned some into my mouth to keep myself from getting involved.

'He wants you – we both want you – to have choices in your life,' she went on. 'He doesn't want to make those choices for you. He just wants to be sure that when your results come out, you have whatever you need to do the things you want to do.'

I was making myself sick with the muesli, guzzling it down like there was no tomorrow.

'There are parents out there who are pushing kids into things just to fulfil their own childish ambitions. Whatever you want to do is fine with us, so long as you're happy'. The stodge of muesli had lodged in my stomach. I felt bloated.

'I'm not happy,' I said.

She was trying desperately to read my eyes but I shadowed them over with a frown of annoyance.

'It's not school; you're not worried about the exams.'

I didn't answer but she could see I agreed.

'Is it OD? I know we've never talked about fellas and all that, but I've been through these things in my time. You can tell me.'

I don't know why I was shocked by the realisation that May hadn't always been Tom's wife and had known other fellas, other men even, but I was. And once again, I found myself saying something I hadn't even worked out in my head.

'I'm not going with OD, I told you already. I'm going with Seanie Moran now.'

'That's all very sudden,' she said.

'It's not sudden. Don't tell me Seanie is unsuitable too.'

'I never said OD was unsuitable, did I?'

'Tom did.'

'Tom bent over backwards for OD. It's not his fault that OD didn't want to know.'

'I don't want to hear about OD,' I said angrily. 'And I didn't burn my books because of him. Do you take me for a Boyzone groupie or something? My life isn't ruled by fellas and it never will be.'

Then, just as we were edging towards the real story, the phone rang.

'I'll get it,' I said. I rushed out, beating Tom to the phone by inches.

At the other end of the line, Seanie had to repeat his 'hello' three or four times before I got my racing heartbeat in check.

'Seanie, any luck?'

'You won't believe it, Nance, but ...' His voice was flat with disappointment.

'Don't tell me he's ...'

'No, no, but he's over in England at some kind of reunion. He won't be back until next Wednesday.'

'I knew something like this would happen,' I said disgustedly.

'Nance, I'll try again on Wednesday but would you think about going back to school in the meantime?'

I knew it was blackmail and I knew he knew it too. But, I thought, at least he cares enough to be concerned for me. He tried again.

'It might be a good idea not to be stuck in the house all day. What do you think?'

'Yeah,' I said and it didn't feel like giving in. 'I'll go.'

He was slow to react and, in the silence, I sensed his nervousness.

'Would you like to come for a drive tomorrow ... somewhere?'

Seanie was one of the few who drove themselves to our school. The car – a beautifully restored, deep green Morris Minor – wasn't his but he got to use it whenever he wanted. If I went, I'd be telling the world that it was over between me and OD. And with the car horn playing 'Tubular Bells' there'd be no hiding from anyone.

'What time will you call?' I asked.

'If you don't want …'

'I'll be ready at half two but I'll have to be back by five, all right?'

'Sure,' he said. 'No problem. That's great. Half two then.'

'This doesn't mean we're … ' I began but wasn't sure what to say next.

'I know … I know what you're saying and it's fine,' he assured me. 'It's fine with me.'

But he didn't really know what I was saying, because I didn't know myself.

OD

'I put it on a plate for him,' I said. 'All it needed was a touch.'

Another Monday morning and I was still mad as hell over Saturday's match. If Seanie had put away the chance I made for him we'd at least have scraped a draw. In front of an open goal he'd duffed it because, as usual, he was too casual. When he shrugged his shoulders after the ball fizzled wide, I could have buried him. To make matters worse, St. Peter's had won their game and we were two points behind.

We were down behind the rockery in the 'secret garden', four of us. Or three of us. Johnny Regan skulked a little way off, smoking his dope, with his ear cocked – waiting for his chance.

When I looked at Johnny, I felt sick – sick with myself. This past year, since Johnny got into the drugs, I'd been protecting Beano from him. I knew he'd already turned some of the lads on to the stuff and Beano was an easy target. Now I was the one who'd led him astray and it made me feel lower than Johnny, if that was possible.

I had a bad feeling about the fact that Beano and Snipe were so late but, for the moment, I concentrated on Seanie.

'He's a lazy bastard,' someone said. We all agreed – all except Johnny, who was busy getting the last drag from his joint.

'Moran's only on the team because he's Mahoney's star pupil,' someone else muttered.

'Too busy studying,' I said, following the stupid logic and taking a look back at the cabin to see if the padlock was off it yet.

Johnny Regan chuckled and said something under his breath as I watched Snipe come in by the gate at the front of the site. When I turned back to the lads to tell them, they'd gone silent and were gaping at Johnny. Then they all looked at me. I picked up a shovel.

'Snipe's in,' I told them. 'What did you say, Johnny?'

He started backing away, keeping an eye on me as his boots crunched on the pebble path. In his hand was a crowbar.

'I said Moran's a busy lad, for sure.'

'Meaning?'

'You said he was too busy studying. I said he was a busy lad, full stop, amen, so be it, end of story.'

I took a step in his direction and he stumbled. The crowbar fell to the ground and he went down on one knee. He looked like he was praying, but the sneer was still on his face.

'What's on your mind, Johnny? Besides that greasy hair.'

Still on the ground, he picked up a fistful of pebbles and shuffled them around in his hand. 'Moran's mind isn't on his game 'cause he's in love, OD.'

I was holding on to my shovel like it was a piece of wreckage after an explosion. 'You saw him with Nance?'

'Yep, up at her house. And yesterday he took her for a ride – in his car.'

I'd accepted the fact that I'd been dumped, but the idea of being dumped for Seanie Moran was too much to handle. I swung the shovel at Johnny and he just about made it out of the way. The blade slashed through the pebbles and dug out a wound of clay. He scrambled like the rat he was on to the grass verge and, lifting himself slowly, spat the pebble dust out of his mouth.

'You're mad, Ryan. It runs in the family.'

He legged it as I pitched the shovel at him, but I wasn't aiming for a hit. I just wanted to get rid of him. I looked around the site trying to figure out what to do next. After a few minutes of standing there like a statue I went over to the cabin to find out where Beano was.

Snipe wasn't reading *The Sun*. He seemed preoccupied and when he saw me he started shifting some papers around his desk.

'Yeah?' he said.

'Where's Beano?'

'Were you with him last night?' he demanded.

That brought out the Judas in me, or the other fellow who said 'Am I my brother's keeper?'

'No,' I lied and slid away – like a snake.

Beano was hungover and probably pretending to be sick; it was as simple as that, I told myself. I went to work, glad to lose myself in the mindless drudgery and keeping well away from Johnny Regan.

At lunchtime I skipped Super Snax. I didn't feel hungry. Instead I went up to Beano's house. Snipe would be down at the bookies.

Beano's mother answered the door. Eventually. She was a small woman with a distracted, half-wild look, but her voice was soft. Behind her the house smelled of disinfectant.

'Could I talk to Beano, Missus?'

'Beano?' She seemed to be having trouble remembering who Beano was. She hadn't opened the door all the way and now she was inching it closed.

'He has the flu.'

Looking beyond me, her eyes were watery, not with tears but with a kind of cloudy mist. I knew from Beano that she was on some kind of tablets for her nerves. That day she must have taken a double dose, she was so far gone.

'The flu … he can't walk. Talk, I mean; he can't talk … or something …'

She was losing me now. She retreated into the hallway, forgetting to shut the door fully. I called up the stairs from the door, hoping Beano would answer and put my mind at rest.

'Beano? Beano? Is everything OK?'

The only sound was from the telly in the front room. She was turning up the volume, drowning out the noise of the world.

'I'll see you tomorrow,' I called, feeling a right jerk shouting into the empty hallway.

I had time to spare before getting back to the site so I dropped in home for a few minutes. I thought I'd grab a cup of tea and read a bit in my room. I'd picked up a biography of Dylan Thomas in the library a while before, but the way things worked out, I hadn't really got down to reading it. I wanted to understand those poems of his better; I thought if I did, I could write something myself. I'd failed at everything else; it seemed like the only thing left to try.

I went upstairs to get the book. From the kitchen I could hear Jimmy's comings and goings, and I passed on the tea. Stretching out on the bed, I forgot the pain in my knee and Beano and Seanie Moran and Nance and all the others. Everything, including time itself.

Dylan Thomas was already eighteen and moving from his native Wales to London when the door of my room opened. It wasn't Jimmy Ryan, not the Jimmy Ryan I knew. His long, oily slick of hair had been shorn to the roots. His tooth-filled grin was no longer ridiculous. He almost looked young. A touch of face-paint to cover the little purple veins on his face, and some padding on the slouched shoulders, and he could have starred as himself in the film of his early years.

'Are you on a half-day or what?' he asked pleasantly.

'No,' I muttered, too stunned to say any more.

'Some morning I had, OD, I can tell you.' He came over and sat on the windowsill by my bed. 'First, the haircut. They could have stuffed a mattress with the clippings!'

It didn't seem to matter to him that I was pretending to read again.

'Then, in I goes to the Sound Centre. "How much," I says, "would a second-hand trumpet set me back?"'

He stopped and I couldn't help looking up at him. When I did, I could see the shadow cross his face. Now his voice wasn't filled with false cheerfulness. It had an edge to it that really surprised me.

'Some little prat from Cork owns the place. Do you know him? Murray?'

The name came out sounding like 'slurry'.

'He says, "Too much," and goes back to stringing an old wreck of a guitar. "I could pay by the week," I says, and he shakes his head.'

I could just imagine Jimmy standing there being ignored by this Murray fellow who I knew well. I'd ordered an early Van Morrison album, *Astral Weeks*, from him a while before. Murray could keep his *Astral Weeks*. Mad as I was at Murray, I was even madder at Jimmy for making little of himself.

'So I ask him what has he got in that line, and he puts down the guitar and he's about to throw me out. I ask him again what has he got and how much is he looking for.'

I put down the book. I didn't like the way this story was going. It sounded like it was going to be another of his hard-luck stories. I wanted to put an end to it.

'What time is it?' I asked, sharpish.

Which was a waste of breath. He was still at the Sound Centre.

'I leaned in over the counter and I says, "Show me the trumpets, son."'

All of a sudden, the tension was gone and he was chuckling to himself so much his false teeth slipped and the illusion of youth was broken for a split second. He laughed it off and, secretly, I was glad he'd been able to. I found I was grinning too. His face lit up when he saw that.

'I think it must have been the skinhead haircut, OD. Murray was wetting himself. Out come the trumpets. Two duds, one beauty – a bit knocked up but shining, boy, shining. I smacked the old lips, got 'em ready.'

He stood up, acting out every move, miming the handover of the trumpet, the fingers testing the stops, raising it up and clearing his throat.

'How much?' I asked.

He puffed out his cheeks, pulled in a big breath, and let it go.

'Sounded like a bull with diarrhoea. There was a phone at the far end of the counter and Murray was looking at it and thinking about scrambling for it. But I got myself between him and the phone and I blew again and I gave him …'

'Jimmy! How much?'

'You should've seen his face. If only I had one of those Scamcorder yokes, OD …'

'Camcorders,' I snarled.

'Yeah, those things. If I had it on tape I'd watch it for the rest of my life. He thought I was a chancer, OD, but I showed him what I really am. A musician. Anyone can sell records. I can make music. I can make music with this boozy old mouth and this … this …'

He was looking at his hands. They were supposed to be holding a trumpet. Only he really believed in the pretence.

'How much will it cost, Jimmy?'

The trumpet that wasn't there vanished. He folded his arms very tightly.

'Don't matter,' he said. 'It's mine. Murray's holding it for me until I get the money together. I gave him a £10 deposit. It's mine.'

NANCE

My first day back at school and I was on my way to the principal's office. But, no, I wasn't in trouble. I'd sat quietly in class all morning and not been asked one question, and that annoyed me. I wondered if Tom had asked them to go easy on me. Now I was going down to meet him and collect the books he'd got together for me. The principal was out so Tom was in charge. I knocked on the yellow-painted door and the sound echoed along the empty corridor.

'Come in,' Tom called from inside and, for the first time in days, he looked pleased to see me.

'I have all your stuff here except …' he began.

'Why are the teachers steering clear of me?' I asked. 'Is that your doing?'

'Of course not,' he said. 'But they're not fools. They add one and one and get two, that's all.'

'I'm sorry I embarrassed you,' I said without feeling.

He put on his hurt father face. I don't know what kind of

face I had on but it had only one meaning for Tom.

'Why all this sudden hate, Nance? If I don't know what I've done wrong, how can I put it right?'

'I don't hate you,' I said, but I was looking at the file cabinet beside him when I said it and not into his pleading eyes.

'Did you talk to your mother?'

'The question made me dizzy until I realised he was talking about May.

'Talk to her about what?' I said, acting the dummy.

'Surely you can tell her what's wrong? I know you can't tell me.'

The filing cabinet was grey and shiny. That was all there was to know about it. But I kept on staring at it anyway. His long sigh told me he'd given up trying to get through to me for now. I turned for the door, forgetting why I'd come in the first place.

'Are you taking the books?' he asked.

'I suppose.'

'Look, Nance,' he said wearily, 'I don't know why you did what you did last week. And I don't know why you came back to school. But I'd prefer if you'd decide one way or the other. Otherwise, I'll have to make up your mind for you.'

'So what's new?'

'What do you mean?'

'Making up my mind for me. You always do that anyway,' I said.

'You know that's not true.'

His hands, which had been moving aimlessly around the cluttered desk, settled on a letter-opener, a miniature Samurai sword. I was thinking of how enthusiastic he'd been when I'd said I wanted to be an engineer. He got books for me and photocopied the pages from the prospectuses of the different colleges. It seemed to me now that he'd found a target for me and was determined to get me there.

'I don't need anyone making up my mind for me,' I told him.

He raised the letter-opener and held it out to me. I didn't know what he was at but it felt scary. I hoped the school secretary or one of the teachers didn't come in and find him like that. He stabbed his finger in the middle of his chest.

'Take it,' he said, 'there's a soft spot just here. If you push this in hard enough you'll kill me. It's sharp enough.'

'I'm going back to my class,' I said.

'I'm sorry, Nance, that was silly, bloody silly. If you don't want to go back in, don't.'

Not wanting any more of this weirdness I let it rest, gathered up my new books and left him. The rest of the morning passed without incident and I spent most of the time trying to figure out what I'd say if I found Heather Kelly. But my mind kept drifting back to those few minutes spent in the office with Tom.

It wasn't the business with the letter-opener that bothered me. When he'd asked if I'd talked to May, I'd thought nothing of it. Now that there was time to think, I wondered if he really didn't know whether I'd spoken to her. If he didn't, did that mean they'd already stopped confiding in each other? I hadn't expected to drive a wedge between them so quickly. I couldn't help thinking that if it could so easily be sundered, then their relationship couldn't have been as perfect as it had always seemed.

Seanie offered me a lift home at lunchtime and I accepted only because I was afraid I'd put him off the idea of helping me. On our spin the day before, we hadn't talked very much. We'd driven down to the Glen of Aherlow and sat in the car for an hour looking out at the view of fields dotted with farmhouses and sheep and cattle. It was so good to feel that you were somehow above all the little problems down there in the world.

Later, we'd dropped into a coffee shop in Tipperary. As we sat drinking coffee and minding our own business, this small kid of three or four came and stood staring up into my face. I smiled at him but he just looked goggle-eyed at me for all of a minute. Seanie got uneasy. He finished his coffee and stood up to go.

'It's getting late.'

Just then, the child ran back to his parents who were sitting nearby. 'That girl is all brown,' he yelped.

They tried to hush him up but he went on enthusiastically.

'And her hands is all brown on the back and all white on

the front!' he cried. His parents pretended to tie the child's shoelaces. It was almost funny how they got in each other's way, as they ducked for cover.

'He's just a dumb kid, Nance,' Seanie whispered.

I didn't like his hushed, secretive tones. I didn't like being reassured. I didn't like the look in his eyes that said he was suffering on my behalf. 'Seanie, I don't need anyone to tell me not to take this kind of stuff to heart,' I said. 'I know the story. The story never changes.'

I felt sorry for that couple as I remembered the incident, and I felt sorry for having been so hard on Seanie. I knew it wasn't fair to be so silent as he drove me home but I had nothing to say to anyone. We pulled up at the front gate and I opened the car door.

'Will I collect you on the way back?' he asked over the sound of REM on the car radio.

'"Night Swimming",' I said, 'what does it mean? That song?'

'I haven't a clue,' he answered, 'but it sounds good.'

Then I realised I wasn't asking Seanie the question. I was asking OD. He always had a theory about every song, film, book you mentioned. I'd usually disagree just for an argument – the kind of argument that kept us together, not the other kind that drove us apart. We could sort of show off to each other and prove we weren't just another lovestruck couple, interested only in kisses and sweet nothings – though we had plenty of those too. It would never be like that between Seanie and me. None of that talk, none of those kisses.

I looked over at him. Good-looking as he was, I wondered how I could have led him on – though, of course, deep down I knew well why. I couldn't wait until Wednesday, when I wouldn't have to keep up this pretence with him any longer.

There was a moment of panic when I imagined he was moving towards me but he was just turning the radio volume down. He didn't seem to have noticed my scramble to get out.

'We'll find her, Nance,' he said. I could almost hear the handcuffs clicking on my wrist – we were in this together now, that was how he saw it.

'Yeah.'

'Will I collect you after lunch?'

'No, I'll walk,' I said. 'Clear my head.'

I waited for the Morris Minor to pull away out of sight before turning from our front gate and heading for De Valera Park. Passing by OD's house, which I could have avoided but didn't, I wondered if Jimmy had made any progress with his big comeback plan. I hoped he had, though the evidence of the still overgrown front lawn and the unrepaired front door wasn't promising. OD, I supposed, had got to him and shaken his new-found confidence. The thought was almost enough to turn me back from Beano's house.

I was going there because I wanted to tell Beano – and,

through him, OD – that Seanie wasn't the cause of our split, that there was nothing between Seanie and me. I didn't want OD believing the rumours that were sure to have spread. Not because I wanted to get back with him, but because I didn't want him or anyone else thinking I was some kind of bimbo, running from one fellow to the next.

The nearer I got to Beano's, the less sure I was that this was the real reason and the less sure I was of what I was going to say. Maybe I'd just ask how OD was. Maybe that was all I wanted to ask.

I'd have walked right by the house if the front door hadn't already been open and if I hadn't heard what my ears could scarcely believe. Mrs. Doyle was at the door before I got to the knocker. She didn't look well. In the background, Beano was crying out loud.

'What do you want?' she screeched. 'Will ye all just shag off and leave us alone!'

'What's wrong with Beano?' I asked, quaking but firm.

'He busted his ankle. It'll mend. I wish I could say the same for my head.'

'Did you call a doctor?'

'I been to a hundred doctors. All they do is give me tablets.'

I wondered whether she even heard the racket from upstairs. The pain of Beano's cries was slicing through my brain.

'For Beano!'

I didn't realise I'd shouted until Snipe appeared behind

his wife. I don't know who he expected to see, but from the look on his face he seemed relieved it was only me. He put on a stupid, ingratiating smile.

'His bite is worse than his bark,' he said, raising his eyes in the direction of Beano's cries.It was supposed to be a joke but I shivered at the coldness of a father making fun of his son's pain.

'Has he had a doctor?' I demanded.

He scowled. He knew how much he disgusted me.

'He's been taken care of,' he said. 'Not that it's any of your business. What the hell is going on here anyway? First Ryan comes and then you …'

I felt a strange sensation when I heard that OD had been here before me. It was like we were still headed in the same direction, the two of us, only arriving at different times.

Pushing his wife aside, Snipe caught hold of the door and slammed it in my face. As I stood there waiting for Beano's next cry, a cry that didn't come, I realised that tears were streaming down my face. *I can't help you, Beano*, I was telling myself; *I can't even help myself.*

There were voices on the street behind me and I was too ashamed to turn from the door. I wanted to fall to my knees. I wanted someone to pick me up. When I heard the car horn I knew it was blowing at me. The sound was unmistakable: the first few bars of 'Tubular Bells'. I ran to the Morris Minor and got inside as fast as I could.

I buried my head in my hands. When I found my voice,

I talked and talked. I told Seanie why I had to find Heather Kelly – the whole story, from the moment I'd come upon the photo. Everything. It took the best part of an hour and I never lifted my eyes once. We missed two classes but Tom never said a word. I suppose he was glad I went back for the last two – if he cared at all now about me and school.

But I forgot about Beano. I never said one word about Beano. Maybe I thought OD would sort it out. In a way, I was right.

OD

When you think things can't get any worse, that's when you can be sure they will. Call it OD's Law if you like – disaster plus X (the unknown, the future, the next minute) equals double disaster. That afternoon, as I left Jimmy in his fantasy world where money didn't matter, I was lower than zero. Then I shot down the minus scale.

I was at the gate before I copped Seanie's puke-green Popemobile parked near Beano's house. I couldn't make sense of the scene. It was like seeing a hearse outside a disco or something off-the-wall like that. Seanie wasn't looking in my direction but staring worriedly at the passenger seat. Next thing I saw Nance's head appear. I didn't wait to see her face. I staggered back towards the house like I was going home after a night at the Galtee Lounge. I went out the back way by the lane behind our house.

My heart was banging out a mad beat somewhere between reggae, rap and house. The lyrics went something like 'It doesn't matter' or 'So what', but they didn't fit the rhythm. At the same time, someone must have been sticking pins into a little effigy of me because my knee was peppered with stinging jabs.

Blaming Seanie came easily. If he hadn't moved in so quickly, maybe we would have got over this little glitch. All the way back to the site I was struggling between being tempted to give him a hiding and telling myself to get on with my life. Which wasn't much of a choice, given the lousy life I had.

Call it a life? What was I? A drop-out, a boozer at seventeen, half-crippled, a few weeks left before I was back on the dole permanently – terminally. I pushed in the gate of the park, my mind hovering somewhere between lashing out and letting it all just die.

Snipe wasn't waiting for me, in spite of the fact that it was well after three. I passed in front of the cabin and he was so engrossed on the telephone that he didn't even look up at me. Getting a late bet on, I guessed. I headed over towards the rockery. Then I saw the two surveyors: one was looking into a thing like a camera on a tripod and taking notes; the other one, standing a little way off, stood holding a long white stick marked off like a ruler.

I drifted over to where the lads were looking busy shifting wheelbarrow-loads of pebbles from one spot to another and then back again.

'What's going on?' I asked, but no one seemed to know.

It didn't feel right but I didn't know why. I knew next to nothing about building and all that stuff, but I knew there was something dodgy about surveying a site when the job was nearly finished. And why would you want to survey an amenity park anyway?

For whatever reason, paranoia or just wanting a blow-up, I marched over to the cabin. Snipe was off the phone and in such a state he was almost bouncing up and down on his seat.

'What do you want?' he rasped.

'Don't tell me,' I sniggered. 'You lost a fiver on the two-thirty at Ketterick.'

'Beat it, OD.'

I sat on his desk just to send his blood pressure up a few notches. He was too interested in watching the surveyors outside to make his usual protest.

'I was wondering what those fellows were doing out there,' I said.

'You were wondering, were you?' he said, but he still seemed distracted. 'The Boy Wonder.'

He looked at the site plan on his desk and rubbed his chin roughly with his hand.

'We messed it up, did we?' I asked.

'Clear off, OD.'

'It's only a bloody park. What does it matter if we screwed it up a bit?'

'We didn't … I didn't screw it up. Everything was done by the book. Everything, down to the last pebble.'

'So what's the problem?'

'The problem is no one will tell me what the problem is. Now get back to work. I've some more calls to make.'

I was at the door before I remembered Beano. It wasn't a good time to ask and I was going to leave it until he called after me.

'And Ryan?'

'Yeah?'

'Stay away from our house … you and that young one of yours.'

'Nance?' I asked, genuinely puzzled.

'The black one. Just call her off, right?'

He made 'black' sound like a four-letter word. I went back to the desk, but this time I circled around to his side.

'Nance is not my "young one". But I'm warning you, don't talk about her like that.'

He was getting nervous but putting a brave face on it.

'I said she's black and black she is. What's your problem, son, are you colour-blind or what?'

'No, I'm not. I can see you're a little pink man.'

He shifted his weight on the chair and I could see he was thinking about having a go at me. I egged him on.

'And I'll call to Beano any time I feel like it,' I said. 'He's my friend.'

He shot up and grabbed my shirt-front. Before I knew it I was pinned up against the wall. I had to push hard three or four times to get him off me.

'You filled him with drink, you gurrier,' he shouted. 'Do that again and you're dead meat!'

I might have laid into him then but I knew he was right. I was so sick with myself I found myself muttering an apology to Snipe. Truly, I was out of control.

'I'm … I'm sorry about that … I … shouldn't have …'

He was even more taken aback than I was. He fixed his rugby tie and straightened out the sleeves of his jacket.

'No point in being sorry now, boy, the damage is done.'

I got myself out of there before I lost my head completely.

There was only an hour left before clocking-out time but the minutes were like centuries. I found a huge rock we'd discarded from the rockery and grabbed a lump hammer. Disregarding the strange looks from the lads and Johnny Regan's wash-eyed leer, I smashed it to pieces and buried the pieces in the earth with my hammering.

At home, three-quarters of an hour later, I was sure I'd calmed down. I left Jimmy alone about the trumpet money and, for a change, I made the tea – not that there was anything very complicated about buttering some bread, which was all we ever had in the house those days. I went to the local chippers and Jimmy dined at home – on take-aways. The only food smell in our house was from vinegary chips and I hadn't noticed the absence of that smell at the time. If I had, I'd probably have put it down to the overwhelming mock-lavender odour which he was adding to every day on his daily round of household chores.

I was so calm that I actually asked him if the bleeding in his gums had eased. He was glad I asked.

'No problem, OD. We're on the ball, boy, on the ball.'

He was laying on the cheerfulness a bit thick and I was afraid that, by going on about the money earlier, I'd put him off the whole 'comeback' idea. I wasn't able to say it but I did want him to succeed. If I'd been half-decent about it, I'd have tried to give him a boost. Which, of course, I didn't. Instead, I went up to my room and got back into Dylan Thomas and followed him around the pubs and publishers of London. My hero was on his way to fame and alcoholism. Which, back then, seemed better than the anonymity and alcoholism that was Jimmy's lot – and mine.

At around seven, I got my gear together and left the house to go training. Even after Mahoney took over the team I still got a buzz from jogging, sprinting, practising set-pieces and all the general messing and craic of those Tuesday and Thursday nights. Now, the thought of doing in my knee altogether in a kickabout or something had spoiled all that for me. Each session was just another stage in the obstacle course my life had turned into.

Still, I knew I had to show up. Mahoney was a stickler for playing only those fellows who trained. On the previous Saturday he'd been in a foul mood even before the Cashel match. So there was no question of even trying to make excuses. I had to go.

All went well for a while. We did our laps and exercises

under the two floodlights I'd actually helped Mahoney to put up. When he'd said I was good at that kind of stuff, he hadn't made it sound even remotely like a compliment. He'd made a lot of changes in the way we trained and played, and our results proved him right. I had to give him credit for that much. He'd played in the League of Ireland with Bohemians back in the early 70s and he knew what he was about. We'd been second to bottom the year before; we were now second from the top.

The going was tough, and I was being as careful as I could without letting it show too much. Which was fine until the seven-a-side started. Usually Seanie and me were put on the same team and we rarely lost. When Mahoney landed us on opposite sides I despised him enough to believe he knew I had it in for Seanie. It felt like a trap.

I was getting nowhere up front. The service was lousy and even if it hadn't been, I was being way too cagey. At the other end, Seanie was knocking them in for sport. Bad loser that I was, I started slagging off some of our defenders and got the usual answer: 'Shut your face and get some goals!' I started coming back towards the halfway line trying to pick up some ball, and the closer I got to Seanie, the more I was tempted to do him.

Finally, my chance came. He was gliding in from the left and pushed the ball too far in front of him. I slid in with the good leg and took him from the knees down. He stayed down, clutching his shin, and I looked around instinctively for Mahoney. No sign of him. I'd been lucky – for a change. From behind me, I heard a voice mutter, 'There's no call for that, OD. He's our best player.'

I whipped around to see who'd said it but quickly decided I'd made a big enough ass of myself already. Seanie got to his feet with blood showing through his otherwise perfectly white socks. It didn't seem like some big showdown any more. The fight was gone out of me.

'Can we talk, OD?'

That was the last thing I expected Seanie to say.

'About what?' I said 'You want some tips on how to handle Nance?'

'You've got it all wrong about me and Nance,' he insisted. 'Anyway, that's not what I want to talk about. It's about that job in the park … You're wasting your time there.'

'It's none of your business what I do with my time.'

'Get yourself out of it before it's too late, OD.'

I was so hyped up I wasn't even beginning to ask myself the right questions. Like: why the sudden interest in my future? Any fool could have added this one and one and one and got three. Moran's visit to the park when he knew well Snipe wouldn't be there; Snipe's concern over the two surveyors; Seanie's big hint. Any fool but me.

NANCE

What happened over the next few weeks I can only describe as a kind of stop-go roller-coaster ride. I'd get to the crest of a climb, whoosh downwards, and then it would turn into a freeze-frame. Nothing would happen for days and then I'd be flying again. And all the time there was this feeling of excited panic, but not the happy carnival kind. At home, the atmosphere was becoming unbearable. At first, it seemed as if Tom and May had separately agreed that he was to blame. May told me again and again that Tom had never meant to make me feel I had to live up to some impossibly high standard he'd set for me. She said this so often I began to wonder if it was herself and not me she was trying to persuade.

'Don't be afraid to tell the truth,' she'd say. 'Tom will understand.'

Tom said something very similar, but he was somehow half-hearted about it. He seemed just to be going through the motions.

'I'm prepared to admit I put pressure on you, Nance, but I didn't mean to,' he'd say. 'If we could just talk about it … '

Slowly, however, a change came about in both of them. As they seemed to drift further away from each other this strategy of theirs came apart. May withdrew from me altogether and barely spoke to me at all. She threw herself completely into her painting and jewellery-making.

In a funny way, Tom was closer to me during those weeks. But it was the kind of closeness I didn't want. It was like having a kid brother who's constantly hanging onto you when you just want to be left alone. If May had stopped trying, Tom was trying too hard.

He began to encourage me to go to the pictures, even to discos, sometimes even on week nights. This wasn't his usual style. He'd never objected to me going out but there had often been an air of disapproval as he handed over the money for these things in the past. Maybe it had something to do with OD and Seanie, but now it was a fiver and all smiles. I refused all the offers, and finally I told him to leave me alone. He didn't lose the rag over it. I suppose he was too devastated.

'I've failed you, Nance,' he said. 'I've failed you.'

If my intention had been to bring him to his knees then I'd succeeded. Instead of feeling any remorse I just got more angry. It was an anger that came out in petty ways – door-slamming, silly disagreements over trifles. In the end, my anger was matched not by Tom but by May.

Tom had made his speciality, lasagne, for dinner. I pushed my plate away, telling them spitefully I didn't want to get BSE from the mince in it. Of course, I knew he always used minced lamb, which was supposed to be safe, but BSE was the last thing on my mind.

May had been sprinkling salt on her plate and she slammed the salt cellar down on the table. It was one of those little glass ones; as a child, I'd decorated it with tiny shells from a play set I'd got for Christmas. The little shapes which were once so beautiful to me and which had survived the years fell away and skittered around the table. She didn't speak until the last one stopped rocking back and forth and our eyes met.

She was a decibel away from screaming when the words finally broke through.

'We've taken all we can of this, Nance,' she said. 'We've tried to be reasonable but you treat us like dirt. You think you can get away with bloody murder, with carrying on like a – '

'May …' Tom said, trying to stop the flow. She silenced him with a look that was very close to hate.

'It has to be said. You're destroying us, Nance, you're – '

'May,' he pleaded, 'don't do this. Don't blame her.'

They'd turned on each other quite openly now and I couldn't bear it. I shouted, 'Stop it! I'm back at school! What more do you want?'

They fell silent and, standing there, I realised the terrible power I had over them. It was a power much greater than any they'd ever had over me. It was a power I didn't want to have, but there was nothing I could do about it.

I couldn't bring myself to release them from their pain. I couldn't trust them with the truth because I couldn't be sure they wouldn't warn Heather Kelly off once they knew I wanted to meet her.

I went to my room and took out my European history book with its fresh, pulpy smell and its stamp on the cover: specimen copy. All my books were specimen copies now.

The strange thing was that I had got back to studying again. Somehow, I found it calmed my mind down, especially when the disappointments came during the search for Heather. It also kept me from thinking about OD and comparing him to Seanie. These comparisons only led to more guilt – the guilt of stringing Seanie along when I knew I'd never feel for him what I felt for OD. What made the guilt so unbearable was the fact that Seanie was such a nice fellow; he would have done anything for me and he never looked for – well, any reward, of any kind. He just wasn't like that. Maybe it just comes down to the simple, unpleasant fact that, in many ways, 'nice' is plain boring. When I think of all the assumptions I made about him back then, it almost makes me laugh – at myself.

The story of our search for Heather Kelly is as chaotic and farcical as everything else that was happening at the time. It began, as we'd planned, with Seanie's phone call to the old priest, Father O'Brien, on the Wednesday he was to be back from his reunion in England.

For some reason, Seanie hadn't called up to see me on his way back from training on the Tuesday evening. I wondered if he was having second thoughts about helping me. But next day, he was all apologies and said he'd be ringing Father O'Brien at seven. At five past seven I was waiting beside the phone at home and hoping Tom or May wouldn't find me hovering there or hear what was going on. I had to wait five minutes but it seemed like five hours. I picked up the phone before the second ring.

'Seanie?'

'Well, I got him, all right,' he said.

'And?'

'He was a bit confused. He seemed to think Tom was married to Heather Kelly,' Seanie explained. 'Maybe I mixed him up at the start. When I mentioned May he remembered.'

'Does he know where Heather is?'

'No, but he's sure her father had a chemist shop in Limerick. In the city, he thought.'

I was getting shaky now. I couldn't think what to say. It seemed, for a moment, that it was going to be easy. Too easy.

'The thing is, I looked up the phone book,' Seanie said, 'and there's no Kelly's Chemists in Limerick.'

I was plunging down again after the small, fearful high.

'Unless,' he suggested, 'they sold up. We could go over to

Limerick on Saturday morning and ask around. Some of the other chemists might remember.'

I couldn't release Seanie just yet. How could I get to Limerick except in his green Morris Minor? So early on Saturday morning we were on our way. Seanie had to be back for a cup match at half past two.

That morning he really opened up to me about his future. He was having doubts about doing accountancy and he talked passionately about how he'd always wanted to do medicine. Unfortunately, I was totally tensed up, though I did try to encourage him.

When he got more specific about why he wanted to be a doctor, I blew a fuse.

'What I'd like to do is work in the Third World,' he said. 'I want to help –'

'The little niggers,' I snapped, angry that Seanie was turning out to be another of those interfering do-gooders and suspecting that his helping me, this lost black soul, was a kind of try-out for the real thing.

'Nance, it has nothing to do with their ... their colour.'

'I'm just nervous,' I told him. I wished he'd change the subject but he needed to put the record straight.

'Dad says that famines and all that, they're a natural way of controlling the population,' he explained. 'But I can't understand how you can be happy when other people are starving and dying for want of clean water and simple medicines. It doesn't make sense to me.'

The strange tag, the 'Third World' – so weird, so science fiction-like – only served to deepen the sense that, somehow, I didn't belong. My life here was the same as everyone else's: same school, same hang-outs, same day-to-day routine. But in the end, had I more in common with the people of that other world? Would life be better there for me? Simpler, maybe more harsh, but the life I was meant to live? There were no easy answers to these questions. No black and white answers, I thought, and couldn't even raise a smile at my own joke.

We'd reached the outskirts of Limerick by now. In the silence filled only by the low hum of an Oasis tape, I looked for the name 'Kelly' over shop doors and tried to forget what I'd said.

Finally, he said, almost in a whisper, 'Maybe you're right, maybe I should stick to accountancy.'

'Do what you want to do, Seanie,' I said. 'Forget about your father – and me.'

'I can't do that.'

I didn't ask whether he meant he couldn't forget his father or me.

Seanie had a list of chemist shops and we decided to split up. I took the ones around the city centre and he drove away to cover the ones further out. It proved to be a long, frustrating morning. I'd more or less given up hope when, at ten to one, I found myself in one of those few chemist shops that hadn't been modernised.

The old floor tiles, with their emblem of a snake twined around a pestle, were faded from years of use. Behind the high, dark-timbered counter were banks of small, narrow drawers; each one had its ceramic label inscribed with a Latin name in slender black Gothic lettering. Among the garish boxes of headache tablets and sticky plasters stood an array of ancient medicine bottles of all sizes, colours and peculiar but somehow beautiful shapes.

The tinkling of a little bell over the door still filled the air as a tall, grey-haired old man with a slight stoop emerged from behind a timber partition at the counter.

When he asked if he could help me, I had a feeling straight off that I'd come to the right place. I felt like I needed some kind of explanation for wanting to find Heather, and a story came into my head right there on the spot. I was organising a 21st-wedding-anniversary party for my parents and I wanted to get all their old friends together for it. The man – Mr Carroll, 'but call me Michael' – leaned on the counter and listened as I dressed up my lie with truths and half-truths. He must have wondered why I was talking so much. I was wondering the same thing myself.

'We were great old friends, John Kelly and I,' he said when I finally paused for breath. 'Isn't it terrible how people lose touch with each other?'

'So you wouldn't know where he is now?' I asked despondently. 'Or Heather?'

Whether he was trying to remember where the Kellys had

moved to, or just recollecting the good old days when he and Heather's father were young men, I didn't know, but he took his time about answering.

'It must be, what, a good twenty years since John left Limerick. You see, his wife, Nora – a lovely, lovely woman – well, she died and he was never the same after. He sold the business and went to live in Dublin and three years ago, or was it four, he moved to England, to Nottingham. His daughter lives there, you see.'

'Heather?'

'No, no, I'm confusing you now, I'm sorry.' Michael smiled. 'There were two daughters. Celia was the older one and she married over there. As for Heather, the last I heard of her was that she was teaching somewhere outside Galway. That would have been after she came back from Africa in the early eighties, I think.'

'But you wouldn't know exactly where?'

'I'm afraid not, but I could find out. Sure, I'd have to, it's such a nice thing you're doing for your mother and father.'

I squirmed to think of how I'd lied to this decent man.

'Would you leave a phone number?' he said. 'I'll ring you if I come up with anything.'

I did. I thanked him and left with a sour taste in my mouth, but as I hurried back to meet Seanie at the car park, the self-disgust turned to anticipation. I was getting somewhere at last.

Over the next ten days we drew up another list, this time

of schools in County Galway, and started to ring around. Lunch hour most days was spent dialling number after number. Then on the Friday of the week after Limerick, lightning struck – twice.

I'd tried two schools and punched in the number for another in the draughty, evil-smelling phone booth. This one was a national school in a place called Sherrivy. The line was very bad and to make things worse there were the screaming echoes of children's voices in the background.

'Heather Kelly,' I repeated. The man's voice which answered sounded like it came from the bottom of a barrel.

'Miss Kelly? I'll get her for you.'

I slammed down the phone, shaking with terror, and stupidly said 'No!' when it was back in its cradle.

Seanie could see something was up from fifty yards away when I went in by the school gate. He tried not to run as he hurried towards me through the crowd returning to classes.

'Sherrivy,' I said. 'She's in a place called Sherrivy. I forgot to ask where exactly it is.'

'We'll find it,' he said.

At eight o'clock that evening, Michael Carroll rang. He hadn't located Heather, he said, but he gave me her sister's phone number in Nottingham. I wrote it down, though it didn't seem to matter now. I thanked him again for taking the trouble.

'I hope you find her for your parents' sake,' he said. 'It would be a grand surprise for them.'

I said it would. When he rang off I went back up to my maths problems and lost myself in them. I didn't tell Seanie about the call.

On the following Wednesday we headed for Galway. He'd insisted, against all my protests, on taking a day off. We could have waited till the next week when we had a three-day break, but he wouldn't hear of it. As we pulled out of town, he said mysteriously, 'I told him.'

For some reason, OD's name leapt into my mind.

'Told who what?' I asked suspiciously.

'Dad. I told him I was doing medicine,' he said. 'And I told him … some other things … about myself.'

I was really happy for him, and I felt I'd done something to repay his concern for me.

'That's brilliant,' I said. 'How did he take it?'

'I don't think he likes me very much any more.'

He went quiet for a while. Then he pushed a tape into the deck. The car exploded into a cacophony of unmistakably African music. A driving rhythm, big drum beats with a bass line that sent shivers through me.

'What is it?' I asked.

'It's from Kenya,' he explained. 'I bought it last year in Dublin.'

I lost myself in the hypnotic beat, wondering why it had never occurred to me to seek out the music of my native country. We listened to it over and over and Seanie drummed on the steering wheel, enthusiastically familiar with every turn of the rhythm.

The school in Sherrivy, fifteen miles outside Galway city, was one of those old grey stone-built ones; it had long windows and a little stone plaque with the year '1908' chiselled into it. My stomach was suddenly unspeakably empty. That's how I imagine real starvation: an emptiness that is so hopeless it no longer wants to be filled.

'I can't go in,' I said. I didn't even pull away when Seanie took my hand.

'I'll go,' he said.

He was in and out of the school in less than five minutes. He slumped into the driver's seat. I panicked.

'She doesn't want to see me!' I cried.

'Nance, there's a Miss Kelly in there but it's not Heather, it's Helen.'

'I'm sorry,' I muttered in desolation. 'It was a terrible line, I …'

'The thing is, though, she knew Heather about ten years ago.'

I was coasting upwards again.

'Heather left teaching,' he told me. 'She's a librarian now. Somewhere in the Midlands.'

If this was a search for a needle in a haystack, the haystack was getting bigger. But again, Seanie reassured me. Helen Kelly was going to ring around and ask about Heather. She had his number.

'This is crazy, Seanie,' I said. 'You have more important

things on your mind. Let's just leave it.'

'I'd do anything for you, Nance,' he said. 'You're …
you're a good friend.' He spoke as if he'd never had a friend
before, good or bad. But I wasn't a good friend. I was still
holding back. I couldn't even bring myself to tell him about
Michael Carroll's call. I had to have that secret, any secret, to
prove there was an impassable distance between us.

All the way home, we played the Kenyan music. Most of
the time I was trying to figure out what I'd say to him when
we reached town. I was very close to telling him I didn't want
to see him any more but, in the end, I wasn't able to. All I
said was, 'You shouldn't bother with me. I'm not worth it.'

'Don't be silly,' he said. He pulled out the tape, put it in
its case and handed it to me.

'I can't take it,' I said.

'Please, Nance.'

I couldn't refuse. I leaned towards him and kissed him on
the cheek. He looked at me – as if he knew it was the wrong
kind of kiss – the way Christ looked at Judas, I suppose.

I'd told Tom and May we were going up to the university
in Galway, that Seanie was meeting someone in the medical
faculty there. Tom thought it would be a good break for me
now that I'd started studying again. May had said nothing.
We really were miles apart by then. When I got home they'd
both gone out. I rang Celia Kelly – my aunt.

It soon became clear to me that Celia didn't like her sister very much. Her tone was dismissive, and she didn't even bother to ask who I was.

'I haven't seen or heard from Heather,' she declared in a grand accent, 'since she came back from Africa.'

The words, 'Heather' and 'Africa', she spoke with equal distaste. Then she hung up – just like that. I was stunned. Heather, she seemed to imply, had gone astray in Africa. I was the result of that going astray, and to be thought of like that enraged me. I wanted to ring that woman back and tell her what I thought of her, but Tom came back and, without knowing it, saved me from myself. I even managed to swap some small talk with him. For all his faults, he didn't look on me in that sickening way.

Right through the next week, Seanie was on for ringing Helen Kelly in Sherrivy to see if she'd come up with anything. I argued against it, inventing all kinds of reasons, but the real reason was obvious even to him, I suppose. Pain. The pain of drawing nearer to Heather was like flying into the sun; it was blinding me, burning me up.

And every night of that week, that dream came back to haunt me. The dark hideaway, the raised voices, the big bang that left me writhing in sweat and afraid to go back to sleep.

Then, on the Friday, the big farce ended. Helen Kelly rang Seanie. Seanie rang me.

'She's in Waterford!' he exclaimed. 'In the City Library. I told you we'd find her!' He'd already rung the library and asked if she'd be working next morning. She would be.

'I'll pick you up at nine,' he said. 'Nance, are you still there?'

We spend weeks running and ringing around the country and all the time she's less than an hour's drive away.

'Nance?'

'Yeah, nine is grand,' I said. 'And thanks, Seanie … for everything.'

'You too.'

I put down the phone and I thought, *OD, why can't you be like Seanie?*

OD

Things were going from bad to worse. It was like a poem of Yeats's we'd done in school once. 'Things fall apart, the centre cannot hold.' And it wasn't only me and the Nance situation. It was Jimmy and Beano and my crocked-up knee and even the park, which shouldn't have mattered to me but did. More than I could have imagined.

With Jimmy, the falling apart was slow; but I was watching him more closely than ever before, so I noticed more. When the flights of fancy had come to him in the past, his mood would swing about all over the place. One minute he'd be on a high, next minute he'd be shouting and then he'd be mooching in a corner, his eyes spinning with beer.

These days there was no beer, no shouting, no highs. He just got lower and slower. Every movement was an effort. Sometimes, when he started to stir from his chair to make tea or something, it was like watching a trapeze-artist getting ready to jump; I was holding my breath waiting for him to fall or sink back. Slow as he got, he never did sink back. It might take him five minutes to get to his feet but he'd always succeed. Once in a while, I asked him what it was he wanted because the torture of watching him was too much.

When I saw the blood-stained tissues start to show up again, I couldn't take any more.

'Take the shaggin' teeth out, will you,' I raged, 'or go to the dentist.'

The look he gave me cut me in two. I don't think he meant it to. It was a look that said 'Nothing can touch me any more', and it was very like a smile.

A few days later, I came in from work and found him standing in the middle of the floor like he hadn't a clue where he was. He swayed a bit, but there was no smell of alcohol – only that fake lavender I could smell even when I wasn't in the house. For the first time, I started to be afraid for him.

'I'm a bit dizzy,' he tried to explain. 'When you're sitting down a long time and you stand up it can happen. Did you know that?'

I sat him down and made him his lunch from the bread and corned beef I'd bought, but when I got home that evening he wasn't in the kitchen as he usually was. I went upstairs.

His door was closed but I knew he was in there. I was just about to drift back down to the kitchen with my Dylan Thomas book when I heard a kind of gasp from him. His bed was over by the window. On the windowsill, the sombrero quivered like a thing in pain, buffeted by the breeze coming in by the crack in the window pane. He was lying on the bed, bent double, with his arms clasped to his stomach.

I could barely get the words out.

'What's wrong, Jimmy?'

'The corned beef,' he moaned. 'I think it was the corned beef.'

'I had the same thing as you,' I protested, 'and I'm OK.'

'I didn't mean to blame you, OD. But that stuff never agreed with me. I should've said.'

'Did you take anything for it?'

'I'll be grand,' he muttered. 'It passes.'

I went downstairs and tried to read my Dylan Thomas book. The words on the page weren't making any sense to me. Then I remembered what he'd just said: 'It passes.' Which could only mean it had happened before.

Some instinct brought me out to the back of the house, where the black plastic rubbish bag was. Right there on the top were the two sandwiches I'd made him at lunchtime – not a nibble taken out of either one.

That sent my mind away on another of those mad, self-obsessed loops. Instead of confronting him, I got thick and started thinking that if that was all I got for worrying about him – he throws my sambos in the bin – I wasn't going to bother. Maybe I thought it was the withdrawal symptoms from packing in the drink or that his gums were acting up. Or maybe I never got beyond the point of feeling I was wasting my time trying to treat him right. One way or the other, I let it pass. Of all the mistakes I made in those days, that was probably the worst.

The truth is, I was more concerned about Beano. I hadn't seen him since that night in the Galtee Lounge, and as the days passed into weeks I was getting worried out of my skull. The thing was, he never stayed out of work. He could be asleep on his feet and he'd still clock in.

Beano showed up, at last, on the Tuesday of our last week there. Everything was more or less finished. Snipe had brought in one of Mick Moran's JCBs, just to be sure. I think he just wanted to get a few spins in it and show us how expert he was with the bucket. I wouldn't have minded having a go myself but he wouldn't hear of it.

The first thing I noticed about Beano was the limp. The second thing was that he was wearing a pair of boots two sizes too big for him. Snipe's, no doubt. As soon as he came near me I saw how miserable he looked. So miserable, in fact, that I could almost have believed the story about the flu – if it hadn't been for the limp.

His eyes, always red, were pools of blood. His white hair was flattened to his forehead with sweat. The circles under his eyes were like dark stains. I felt my bad knee wanting to give out under me.

'What's the story, morning glory,' I said casually.

He gave me a Jack Nicholson grin, halfway between The Joker in *Batman* and Mac in *One Flew over the Cuckoo's Nest*

– after Mac had had the shock treatment in the asylum.

'No story, OD,' he said. 'Only the flu.'

'You got the flu in your ankle, did you?'

'I fell out of the bed.' He sounded like he was repeating something he'd learned by heart but didn't really understand.

I brought him up behind the fountain and sat him down out of sight of Snipe's cabin. When Johnny Regan made a move in our direction, I warned him off with a glare. He winked at Beano like they had some big secret going between them.

'Beano? Did Regan give you some dope?' He avoided my eyes. At least, I imagined he did. I couldn't really tell. His eyes were all over the place. His lips twisted into a near-smile.

'Lots of dope in our house, OD … more tablets than a chemist shop.'

I was terrified.

'Did you take something?' I asked. 'Did you, Beano?'

'Naw … not a thing,' he said, sticking out his chest, all macho. '"Tough it out, Beano."'

'Snipe said that, did he?'

Beano nodded. I told him if I saw him working that morning I'd carry him home over my shoulder, and went towards Snipe's cabin. On the way, I collared Johnny. He backed off, but not before I warned him. 'If I see you within an ass's roar of Beano, I'll break both your legs, Johnny. And that's a promise.'

In the cabin, Snipe didn't even bother to hide the racing page of *The Sun*.

'Beano shouldn't be at work,' I told him. 'He's wrecked.'

To my surprise he didn't leap over the desk at me.

'We're all wrecked,' he said.

Then I heard the gate open outside. Those two surveyors were there with their equipment again.

'What the hell are they up to?' he asked himself, not me. 'We're on schedule, but no one seems to be interested any more. And they won't tell me what these fellows are up to.'

Something stirred in the back of my dead brain. It didn't make any particular sense to me but I said it anyway.

'A couple of weeks back, Mick Moran came up here when we were locking up. He wanted to get in here to the cabin and ...'

I was going to say Beano let him in.

'... and I let him in.'

He looked at me like he was doing mental arithmetic – slowly. After a while, I could see he wasn't getting the right answer – or, at least, not an answer he liked. He fixed his rugby tie and stood up.

'Beat it, Ryan.'

'Where are you going?'

'I'm going to see the Town Clerk,' he said. 'And if he won't see me, I'll kick his shaggin' door down.'

Snipe used to be a scrum-half. That's where he got his nickname. Sniping from behind the scrum. Which is exactly what he looked like he was doing as he rushed across the front of the park and out the gate.

I looked around the park and, for the first time, felt a real sense of pride in what we'd achieved there. A kind of glowing, uncomplicated feeling came over me. As I got down to work, I drifted away from reality like a child with a new toy. The toy – the illusion that these past few months had somehow been worthwhile – was all the reality I needed. But toys break. The more you play with them, the sooner they break. I think that's why kids play with the boxes and leave the toys for looking at. Kids have more sense than we have.

During the afternoon, the knee started bothering me. I knew I wasn't going to be able for training, but how was I going to get out of it? The pressure was on our team at this stage. We were slipping and my form was rotten – as was Seanie's. We were out of the cup and the previous week we'd scraped a draw with the bottom team, Hibs. Luckily for us, St. Peter's were having a bad run too and we were one point ahead with two games to play. The other teams were managing to take enough points from each other to leave the title race between St. Peter's and us. I had no choice: I had to go training.

I was hoping Seanie wouldn't be there but he was. He nodded at me as I came into the dressing room. I turned away. Mahoney was there too, pulling on his old Bohs jersey. It still fitted him. I was looking at the big number ten when the sickening inspiration came to me.

'I can't train tonight,' I told Mahoney.

'Are you injured or what?'

'No, Jimmy is sick … I've to get the doctor … I was going to wait until after training but I … I don't think I should.'

By now, I was telling myself to shut up, that it was bad enough to use Jimmy without making a song and dance of it. But the trick, the lousy trick, worked wonders. Mahoney hadn't been so nice to me since I was one of his school 'hopefuls'.

'I'll give you a lift, OD,' he said. 'Which doctor is it?'

'It's all right. He's only up the road. Dr. Corbett.'

'Are you sure? I can throw off the boots, no problem.'

'Thanks all the same,' I said and got myself out of the sock-smelly atmosphere as fast as I could.

Needless to say, I didn't go near Dr. Corbett's. I didn't go home either. I went to the Galtee Lounge. Mahoney sent a message through one of the lads not to bother about training on Thursday and not to worry about my place on the team. I did anyway.

The following Saturday, he did actually pick me. I played well and we won. I didn't score myself, but Seanie and me worked up a chance for one of the other lads to score. For a while, we thought Seanie wasn't going to show up for that match. When he hurried into the dressing-room with five minutes to go, Mahoney gave him the kind of hassle he usually reserved for me. Something to do with Nance, I guessed, but I didn't let myself think about it.

Meanwhile, I was beginning to suspect that Jimmy was on the verge of giving up. There was a terrible stillness about him, broken only by the occasional opening and closing of his hands as he sat in his battered old armchair.

'Why do you keep doing that?' I asked eventually.

'Pins and needles,' he said. 'I have them in my feet too.'

'Can't you go out for a walk or something?'

'I went for a walk … the other day.'

I thought he was trying to be smart until he stirred himself in his chair and leaned forward shakily. Then I knew he was leading up to something.

'Yeah, I went for a walk … I called down to the Sound Centre.'

'For what?'

'I told Murray I had … well, a good few quid put together and would he give me the trumpet and I'd hand over the rest in a few weeks.'

I pictured him pleading with Murray and my stomach turned.

'"No way," he says. The little bastard.'

'You shouldn't have done that.'

The little-boy eyes, among the wrinkles and the broken veins, had tears in them.

'I just wanted to get started,' he said.

I thought I knew better. 'You just wanted to get finished. You want out of that dumb dream, and now you can blame Murray.'

Because he didn't answer, I thought I was right.

After that, I took every chance to dig the knife in deeper.

All he had to do was move a finger and I was on him. Not a day went by but I reminded him of his failures over the years. I even talked about what he'd done to Mam. Before that, I hadn't been able to mention her name to him. I did it now because every night, when I'd stopped mulling over all my other troubles, the same question kept coming back to me. 'Why couldn't she just write?' I didn't even want her back any more. I only wanted to know she was all right.

Nothing I could say provoked him, and that left me even more convinced that it was all over for him – yet again.

A week or so later, I sat in the kitchen alone. It was eleven o'clock on a Friday night. Tomorrow there'd be another game, another struggle to hide my injury from Mahoney. I'd fed the lads at the site some more lies about Jimmy's 'illness' and hinted I mightn't make it for the game – all just to create some dumb impression when I did show up. I'd given the Galtee Lounge a miss because I needed to be as right as I could be for the game. I'd been down at the snooker hall with Beano earlier. He still hadn't come out of himself and I hadn't heard a Jack Nicholson line for so long I thought he must have switched heroes – or, maybe, given up on heroes for good.

I hadn't bothered to turn on the telly and I'd finished the Dylan Thomas book. My own hero, the poet, was dead, and I couldn't square the beauty and brilliance of what he wrote with the sordid end he came to in a New York hotel – not far from where another of my heroes, John Lennon, was shot.

I was sitting in Jimmy's chair and staring at the bottle on the mantelpiece. It was one of those outsize gin bottles and it had always stood in that spot since Jimmy won it in a pub raffle – and emptied every last drop of the gin, of course.

I hadn't pulled the curtains or switched on the light; I sat, numb, in the gathering darkness. The street lamp outside threw its light on the big gin bottle, giving it a strange glow in the dead room. The long neck and the rounded shape below made it look like a tall, imposing figure. A man presiding, priest-like, at some ceremony or ritual. A druid, I thought.

On the mantelpiece, beside the bottle, I noticed a couple of empty matchboxes left there since Jimmy stopped tidying the place. Standing stones, some fallen, some still standing. A rush of nervous expectation went through me.

'The Glass Druid,' I said aloud, and almost looked around to make sure no one was there to hear me. I wasn't exactly sure, but I thought the 'Glass Druid' was alcohol. Drinking was like joining hands with him.

'Joining hands with the Glass Druid,' I said to myself.

All around us, the standing stones appeared, statues that were half-living and half-dead. And then I saw their faces. Nance, Jimmy, Mam, Beano, even Seanie, even Mahoney – and me. The vision was as vivid and as unreal as any dream, but I was wide awake. I was more than wide awake. My mind was opening out as if, for once, I understood everything. None of these stone people could reach me and I couldn't reach them. We were all alone no matter how close we got to someone else. But I was the only fool among them who thought the Glass Druid could help me.

Joining hands with the Glass Druid,
Calling to the standing stones,
The men and women who can't speak to me;
Voices like mine, without sounds, without tones.

In the yellow sodium light from the street, I scrambled around the kitchen and found an envelope and a stub-nosed pencil. I wrote down the four lines. There wasn't time to switch on the light, but I could just about make out the words on the brown paper. I read it through, ten, twenty times. I sat back. My first poem. I felt like I was glowing as brightly as the gin bottle.

I read the poem out loud once and then again. Suddenly, I realised why I was doing it. I wanted these words to be heard. I wanted to explain the mad logic of the thoughts behind them. And then, I knew it wasn't just anybody I wanted to hear my poem. Only Nance.

I threw the envelope in among yesterday's cold ashes in the fireplace and then I lost it completely. I cried like a blubbery baby. The hard man, poet, footballer, street-wit broke down some time around midnight, in a silent house somewhere in a universe whose desolate meaning had hit him right between the eyes like a backfiring rifle.

NANCE

As we crossed the wide, four-laned bridge into Waterford I wished that it was the only way into the city and that it had crashed into the river before we got there. Seanie's Morris Minor moved slowly as the lights delayed the Saturday morning traffic. A little slower and I might have jumped out and started back along the bridge.

Just like on our expedition to Limerick, Seanie had to be back for a match in the afternoon. He seemed as uptight as me and we didn't talk a lot. If Seanie thought I needed quiet, he was wrong. It was the kind of situation when small talk, the weather, the Beautiful South tape he'd brought, even football might have delivered me from the confusion of questions that bothered me.

What was I going to say to Heather? Would she refuse to acknowledge me? Or would meeting her somehow leave me worse off than ever?

The Beautiful South were singing 'Everybody's Talking'

and that's how it felt inside my head.

'I like the tape,' I said, drowning out the inner voices and wishing he'd brought something a little louder and looser – Blur, maybe, or The Prodigy.

His mind wasn't on music.

'Nance? About you and OD … about us … there's something I want to clear up …'

'We'll talk about it later, OK? When this is over,' I said – pleaded, really.

'I just thought it might be better if I …'

'Are you sure you know where the library is?' I said, looking blindly ahead.

'Yeah, I checked when I rang. We'll talk on the way back, all right?'

I wished the library would come into view and I wished, at the same time, that it wouldn't. Seanie, distracted by my evasions, turned down a one-way street and we both jumped a few inches from our seats as a bus sped towards us, blasting its horn and flashing its lights. If we were on edge before, we were doubly so after that. I managed to stop myself from bawling him off but I knew I wouldn't be able to hold back for long. Seanie felt the same way, I suppose.

We pulled in at the library and Seanie let the clutch off before he'd got the car out of gear. It jerked forward within an inch of the red Mini in front. For some reason, I began to laugh. Seanie's doom-laden features relaxed to a smile and finally to laughter as loud and panic-stricken as mine.

'Do you want me to go in with you?' he asked when we calmed down.

'Yeah.'

When we reached the door leading to the main lending area, I said, 'You go in first.' I was using him as a shield to the end. I couldn't help it.

He stepped inside and held the door for me. There were no more than a half-dozen people there, browsing among the shelves. Behind the desk at the far end, two women chatted. One was pale and dark-haired. The other one was Heather Kelly. From this distance, she'd changed very little since that photo had been taken all those years ago. Her hair was cut up shorter but that was the only difference. Even the smile was the same one that had burned itself on to my retina.

'Don't go outside, Seanie,' I whispered as I passed beyond the threshold into the lending area, beyond the threshold from innocence to whatever lay on the other side. 'Wait here, won't you?'

'Course I will. You'll be fine.'

Then the long walk began. I struggled to focus on the woman who'd only just noticed me. In spite of my light-headedness, I saw more clearly with each advancing step the changes the years had made in her face. The strangest thought occurred to me – that it was my approach that was ageing her.

If she was in shock, she was hiding it well. She seemed

quite calm. I got to the desk. Now that the big moment had come, my mouth went dry. I couldn't even swallow.

Heather stood up and motioned me to follow her. I looked back at the door where Seanie was still waiting. I shrugged my shoulders, not knowing what to do. He gestured at me to go along with Heather, who by now had reached a door marked 'Staff Only' and was already halfway through.

When I got inside, she was spooning coffee into some mugs. One had a big red heart and announced boldly 'I Luv U'; the other innocently declared 'Forever Friends'.

'Take a seat, Nance,' she said. My heart skipped a beat.

'Thanks,' I said – or meant to; I'm not sure if the word came out.

This wasn't going according to plan. If a stranger had walked in on us, they would never have guessed that this was the reunion of a mother and child after seventeen long years. I tried to bring some urgency into the situation.

'How did you know who I was?'

'Well, I can't say you haven't changed, can I?' she smiled. 'Maybe it's just instinct.' It was all too light-hearted and easy. She filled the mugs from the kettle and sat down next to me.

'How are Tom and May?' she asked pleasantly.

'Grand. They're grand,' I said, more lost and confused with her every word.

'You lose touch, you know. And life goes on, doesn't it?'

I couldn't keep dodging around the issue any longer.

'Are you my mother?'

At last, I'd succeeded in shaking her. Now I was waiting for the big meltdown that was supposed to have happened five minutes before. Instead, I got a nuclear explosion, mushroom cloud, the whole works, that might have lifted me off my seat if my body hadn't suddenly weighed a hundred tons.

'Good God, Nance!' she exclaimed. 'What gave you that idea?'

'Look,' I said desperately, 'I know you're my mother. I know you're lying to me. Please tell me the truth and I won't bother you again. I just want to hear you say it, that you're my mother.'

I was holding the sleeve of her neat white blouse, not just holding it but grabbing a fistful of it.

'Nance,' she said softly, 'I'm not your mother. I might have been. In fact, you could say I nearly was. But it wasn't to be.'

The answer was too complicated and too sincere-sounding to be untrue. Or else she was a very good actress.

'I was engaged to Tom,' she said. 'Christmas Eve 1978, to be precise. Three months later he and May married.'

'I don't believe you.'

'What have they told you?' she asked.

I gave her the old story about the crash and their adopting me. As I did, she nodded as if to confirm every detail. Then I told her about the photo, about her holding me in it and about the man standing behind her.

'Chris,' she said.

'My father?'

I hadn't expected him to have an English-sounding name. She hesitated and finally nodded.

'Chris Mburu. His people were Samburu, from up north originally, but they'd been in Nairobi for years,' she explained slowly, as if not yet sure whether she should be telling me all this. 'He was a nice guy. Very bright, laid-back. A teacher too, but not in our school.'

Heather began to chew her fingernails. Her face, which had been so open, suddenly seemed to cloud over.

'Look, I shouldn't even have told you about Chris,' she said. 'It's not my place to. You really have to talk to them.'

'I can't.'

'Nance, I have every reason to dislike Tom and May after … you know … but I don't. I can see they should have told you about all this but it's not easy for them.'

'And what about me? Do you think it's easy for me?' I cried. 'Please, tell me who my mother is … or was … or whatever. There was another woman in that photo. Is that … was that her?'

Heather bit her nails anxiously and her eyes avoided mine.

'She was an American. They were just passing through, she and her boyfriend. We didn't really know them, Nance, we didn't want to. They were a bad lot.'

I could see that she was more than uncomfortable talking about the American couple; she was actually afraid, really afraid.

'Talk to Tom and May, Nance. Let them finish the story. That's how it should be,' she said. 'I hate to sound like the old voice of experience but if you don't you'll live to regret it. I know this because I've drifted away from my own family. It wasn't all my fault but I might have stopped the drift if I'd only swallowed my pride.'

I told her that I'd talked to her sister, and about the sense of disapproval I'd heard in Celia's voice, and how I felt that it had something to do with me.

'Nance, my sister is one of those wickedly pious types and my mistake, as she would see it, was to marry unwisely – in her terms, that is.'

She sat perfectly still and spoke without emotion.

'After Kenya, I went to Saudi Arabia, but it's no place for a woman to live, believe me. The veils are bad enough but they won't even let you drive a car, can you believe it! I stuck it out for two years and went down to Tanzania. That's where I met John Duffy. Father John Duffy.'

I was tumbling to her real 'mistake'.

'We fell in love. He left the priesthood and we moved to Zimbabwe. We came back to Ireland in '84 and my family have never spoken to me since. Don't let that happen to you, Nance.'

'So you're not going to tell me about these Americans?' She dragged herself away from her own painful memories and took my hand.

'I can't. All I can say is that there was a crash, Nance. I'm

129

sorry … They'll tell you the rest. Only ask. Do ask.'

My chair scraped along the timber floor and I got to my feet somehow or other. 'I finish at one,' she said. 'We could have lunch.'

'We have to be back home early,' I told her. I couldn't stay angry with her for only telling me some of the truth. 'Seanie has a game. He drove me down here.'

'Your boyfriend?'

'My friend,' I said.

She came to the staff door with me. When I opened it she saw Seanie at the other end of the room.

'Nice-looking fellow,' she declared.

'Yeah,' I said.

'Will you call again?' she asked. 'Tell me how it worked out?'

I nodded, but I didn't think I would.

Two miles outside of Waterford, I turned the car radio off and told Seanie that I really appreciated what he'd done for me but that that was as far it went. There was no row, hardly even a breath of tension. After a while, he said, 'You haven't told me what happened in there.'

He listened intently to every detail. When I'd finished he considered it all for a minute or two.

'She's dead right, you know,' he said. 'You'll have to have it out with them. There's no other way.'

I couldn't believe he was letting my treachery, my blatant using and discarding of him, pass. I wondered if I was capable of loving anyone any more.

'I should have told you the truth about us earlier, Seanie. And not led you on. You deserve better.'

'I deserve nothing,' he half-whispered. 'I'm not so good at telling the truth myself.'

He didn't take his eyes from the road.

'I never … I never talked to Dad,' he confessed. 'All that crap about telling him what I really wanted to do was just … fantasy.'

We kept quiet after that. The journey seemed to take an eternity. I felt desperately sorry for Seanie, but what could I do? We'd soon be going our separate ways and that was it. I tried to think of one last crumb of kindness, one last bit of encouragement I could offer him, but nothing came.

At Cashel, he looked at his watch and cursed softly. He pressed the accelerator to the full and left his foot there.

'Sorry, Nance,' he said as we hit a pothole, 'I can't be late. We're going to be a few short today as it is.'

'Who's out?' I asked, not because I wanted to know but just to pass these last few minutes with him in something other than deathly silence.

'Vincent Morrissey is injured,' he explained, 'and …'

OD, I guessed from his hesitation. As if he knew I'd want to know why, he added, 'His father isn't well.'

I was frightened for Jimmy but I couldn't see that I could do anything for him.

'Do you ever talk to OD these days?' Seanie asked.

'Seanie, that isn't why I don't want to … '

'I know, I know. It's just that he won't listen to me and there's something he should know … about the park … See, my father has plans to – '

'I won't be talking to him. So there's no point in telling me this,' I said impatiently.

I had my own problems; I thought OD could deal with his. That's how he had always wanted it to be, no matter how hard I tried to convince him otherwise. I pushed in the cassette on the tape deck. The Beautiful South, 'I'll Sail This Ship Alone'.

OD

Saturday morning. Grand opening of the new town park. 'Grand' wasn't the word. It has one letter too many and the other four are the wrong ones. There was a daft-looking ribbon on the gate – not the new wooden gate, which never arrived, but the same old creaky metal thing that had been there on our first morning at the site. A platform and some chairs stood near the cabin. There was even a microphone and a dicky little speaker. Unfortunately, no-one showed up except Snipe and his crew. Not the Town Clerk, or the local TD, or even a photographer. Snipe was devastated. After an hour or so of hanging around, we were getting uneasy. Snipe looked like a statue made of wax – and the wax was melting. Even I was worried about the purple colour in his cheeks. We started drifting towards the gate eventually. There was nothing to wait for. We'd been paid off the evening before. Snipe was in the cabin, on the phone. It was a long conversation and it wasn't going well for him.

Johnny Regan was the first to reach the gate but Snipe looked up just before he scooted away.

'Don't go anywhere!' he yelled, not even bothering to put his hand over the phone.

Johnny gave him a two-fingered salute and left. All of the others followed except Beano and me. I only stayed for Beano's sake, not wanting to leave him on his own. We sat down on the chairs at the little platform that was basically a few timber palettes thrown together. I thought about telling Beano about my poem, but he was so lost in himself I knew I wouldn't get through to him. Every so often, a convulsive shiver would shake him and he'd clench his jaw in pain.

'You want to get someone to look at that ankle, Beano,' I said.

'Naw, it's fine.'

I might as well have been talking to myself – it was like talking to those standing stones in the poem I'd thrown away. I looked around, trying to think of some way to cheer him up, and the microphone on its rickety stand gave me an idea. I got up and stood behind it. I found a switch on the side and gave it a try.

'Testing one, two, three,' I said. The screech of it nearly blew my ears off.

In his cabin, Snipe was gesticulating madly at me to leave it alone.

'Ladies and gentlemen,' I continued regardless, 'now comes the moment you've all been waiting for here at the

Academy Awards. Hold on a minute now and let me open the envelope for the nominees in the Best Actor category.'

While I pulled out the stub of an old cinema ticket from my cord jacket I sneaked a glance at Beano. He was getting interested.

'Here we go,' I announced. 'First, there's Johnny Regan – for impersonating a human being.'

Beano grinned and clapped softly and I was away.

'Mr. Mick Moran for his starring role in *The Turd*. Seanie Moran for *Invasion of the Bodysnatchers*.'

Beano was getting enthusiastic. I was getting bitter. I had to cool it down.

'And last, but not least, Jack Nicholson in *Farce at the Park*,' I declared, 'And the winner is … is … Jack Nicholson! Come on up here, Jack!'

Beano looked towards the cabin and thought about it. He got up slowly and came towards me. He wasn't smiling any more. He leaned in to the microphone and staring across at his father – who was still stuck on the phone and past caring about our antics – he said, 'I have no one to thank.'

Then he walked away. He was out the gate before I got over the shock. I went to follow him, but as I passed the cabin I heard a noise like a chair or something being knocked over. First thing that came to my head was that Snipe had had a heart attack. I moved to the door and pushed it in.

The place was wrecked inside. The desk had been up-ended; plans, old copies of *The Sun*, paper clips, biros were strewn around all over the ground. Snipe himself stood at the back wall, tearing posters down and crumpling up every bit of paper he could lay his hands on.

'What's all this in aid of?'

He spun around, holding a fistful of paper like it was a grenade with the pin pulled out.

'Get out,' he yelled.

'You're wrecking the place because they wouldn't take your photo?'

'They made fools of us, OD,' he said in utter desolation. 'They treated us like dirt.'

'They? Who do you mean?'

He sat down on the upended desk. His rugby tie was all over the place but he didn't seem to care.

'This must be some kind of record,' he said. 'A town park that opens and closes on the same day.'

'You mean … they're not going to use the park … after all our …'

'They sold it. While we were slogging away here, they sold it to Mick Moran for a private housing estate. Some bastards, what, OD?'

'The surveyors …'

He nodded. The penny was beginning to drop with me. He picked himself up and went past me. The way he straggled out to the gate, he must have felt like he did in his last game of rugby.

'Will I lock it up?' I called after him.

'I don't care if you blow it up,' he shouted. He kicked the gate for good measure as he left the site.

I searched among the debris for the keys. I was on automatic, not letting myself think about the futility of it all. Under a pile of wasted betting slips I found not one, but two bunches of keys.

The first bunch was familiar, since I'd so often locked up the cabin and gate. The second had one of those key-rings with a family crest on it. The family name was Moran. I looked out at the JCB over near the gate. I put the keys in my pocket and thought, You'll never see these again, Moran. Then I went home to get my gear together for the afternoon match. The second last of the season.

Jimmy was in bed when I got to the house. He never got up in the mornings now so that was no surprise. I'd left my boots in a plastic bag with the mud still stuck to them. I scraped off the sludge into the bag and threw it on the fire grate. Only then did I notice that the ashes had been cleared out – and my poem, on its brown envelope, with them. I didn't care. It was only crap anyway.

I realised that Jimmy must have been up earlier after all. I was going to bring a cup of tea up to him but then I got thick over him throwing out the poem. Which was brilliant logic – I thought it was rubbish but I resented him treating it as rubbish.

The Farce in the Park was followed that afternoon by *The Farce in the Dressing-Room*. Mahoney never showed up.

Which was like the universe being turned on its head. Mahoney didn't do things like that. He bawled us out for doing things like that, for God's sake.

I nearly didn't make it myself. I don't know if it was relief or defeat at being finished with the non-existent park, but when I sat down in front of the fireplace, I dropped off to sleep. I woke at ten to three. The match was starting at three. I got to the dressing room at five to and found Seanie handing out the jerseys. He'd got to number seven. The place went silent when I came in. Seanie looked at me like he'd seen a ghost.

'There's no sign of Tom,' he said. 'We had to pick the team ourselves.'

'And I'm too late?'

I looked around at the others but they pretended to be busy getting togged out. I turned to Seanie again.

'So, I'm not in?' I demanded to know.

'I didn't say that, OD.'

Brian O'Toole, our centre-half, peered out from behind his scraggy red hair.

'What do you expect? You weren't here, right?' I wasn't getting any support and I made for the door. Then I heard Seanie's voice, low but deliberate.

'If OD is out,' he said, 'I'm out.'

There was a general murmur of annoyance. Naturally, I thought they all had it in for me – until I realised they were looking at the fellow who'd been given my place, Sammy

Dunne. Sammy was all right. I felt bad about depriving him of his chance to start a game for a change, and I took it out on Seanie.

'I don't need your sympathy, Seanie,' I snapped. 'Sammy should play. OK, Sammy?'

Sammy shrugged. For him, football wasn't the major deal it was for me.

'Hey,' he said, 'the number nine is yours. Put it on.'

Seanie threw the jersey at me. I'd never seen him look angry before that day. I had more than enough anger to fling back at him.

'Did you know about the park? About the houses your old man is putting up there?'

'I tried to tell you but you wouldn't listen.'

I'd always had this sneaking suspicion that Seanie was afraid of me. Now I felt I'd been wrong.

'You and your old man are chips off the same dirty block,' I said. 'Gangsters and thieves.'

'I never did anything to you, OD.'

'No? Does the name Nance ring a bell with you?'

I was really making an ass of myself and in front of a spellbound audience.

'I'm not going out with Nance and I never was,' he said. 'We're friends, if that means anything to you.'

He wasn't lying, I could tell. In fact, he looked like the one who'd had something stolen from him. Was it possible that Nance had handed Seanie off because she wanted to give me a second chance? Even if it was, the way back wouldn't be easy. I'd have to change, and what did that mean? Going back to school? Giving up the drink? What else? Stop thinking about myself and all my own troubles?

It was the first time I'd considered the idea of starting all over again. Maybe if the circumstances had been different I might have made a decision there and then. That would have saved me, and a lot of other people, a lot of hassle.

I started the game badly and all through the first half I didn't get any better. If Mahoney had been there I'd have been a goner. Seanie was having a bummer too. Just before half-time I missed a sitter. I got away from the sweeper and had only the keeper to beat. The bad knee had nothing to do with the way I fluffed it. The keeper couldn't believe his luck when the ball rolled tamely into his arms.

At half-time, we sat around in a circle complaining as usual about the referee and the bumpy pitch. When I heard Beano's manic voice from somewhere in the distance, I was glad of the diversion and glad he'd shaken off that awful quietness that was so hard for me to deal with.

'Move your goddamn butts!' he yelped. I knew he was on some kind of high because this was Jack Nicholson belting out the orders in *A Few Good Men*.

He came over and squatted beside me. His red eyes were gaping like he'd taken one of his mother's uppers – or one of Johnny Regan's. You could hear his whisper at the other end of the pitch. Seanie certainly heard it, because his head snapped away when I looked over at him.

'Can you believe it, OD? That stuff about the houses in the park. My father just told me.'

'Forget it, Beano,' I said, loud enough for Seanie to pick up. 'They're real scum.'

'No way will I forget it, OD,' he said. 'We can do something about it. I just had this incredible idea.'

I got to my feet and pulled him away from the others, who were all listening in now.

'Did you take something, Beano?' I asked angrily.

'OD, you're always saying that,' he muttered. 'I hate when you always say that. Just because Mammy …'

'I'm sorry. Look, Beano, leave it, all right? There's nothing we can do. Get that into your skull and put it down to experience.'

'There is something,' he insisted. 'My father was telling us at home what happened and …'

The referee blew his whistle for the restart.

' … and he told us that Moran's men were going to level the site on Monday morning with that JCB that's parked up there.'

'So?' I said, impatient to get back into the game.

'So? So we built it, OD,' he declared. 'Why should we let someone else demolish it?'

First thing I thought was that we didn't need any more trouble. Then I started to see his mad logic was dead on. The site was going to be levelled anyway, so why not do it ourselves? Why should we let these people walk all over us? It would just be another admission that we were powerless and had no voice or were too brain-dead to raise whatever whimper of a little voice we had.

'Beano,' I said, 'you're a genius.'

'We'll have to get a few shovels and crowbars and things to wreck it with, won't we?' he suggested.

I was standing at the edge of an abyss, getting ready to jump. I knew I might never make it out again, but I was already in free fall when I answered Beano.

'I can go one better than that, Beano,' I said. 'I have the keys of the JCB.'

I went to the centre circle for the kick-off feeling dangerous but in control. I scored two goals in the second half and Seanie volunteered to go off and let Sammy on. He just couldn't get it together, not like I seemed to have. We won 2-0. We were four points ahead of St. Peter's now and they were playing later in the evening. If they lost, the league was ours.

Even as me and Beano left the soccer grounds, I felt like the game wasn't over yet – and that I was on for a hat-trick.

NANCE

When Seanie dropped me off in the centre of town, the place was crowded as it always is on Saturday afternoons, but I'd never felt so alone. OD was gone from my life and Seanie would soon be too, I supposed, after the brush-off I'd given him for his trouble. Tom and May might as well have been living on a different planet from me – or rather, two separate planets. As for Chris Mburu, I'd lost him almost as soon as I'd found him, along with my mysterious natural mother. Though my instincts had been wrong before, I couldn't believe that the American hippie was my natural mother. Maybe I just didn't want to believe it because of her wasted look and Heather's verdict on her and her boyfriend – 'a bad lot'.

I didn't feel angry with Heather Kelly. After all, she'd told me so much I could see she had to leave something for Tom and May to tell. I suppose she thought that the final piece of the puzzle might offer us a way to start talking again. And, in a way, my natural mother's identity was hardly even important now. She was dead. I could never meet her. The only prospect was that I might be able to visit her grave and, maybe, meet some of her family. And there were complications there too. Had they even known of my existence? Would they even want to know? Somehow, all of this seemed a small reward for all I had gone through.

Heather Kelly might have thought that my mother's identity was the final piece of the jigsaw, but I didn't. No, the big question for me was why Tom and May hadn't told me they knew my natural parents. Extraordinary as the whole situation had seemed when I started out, it had turned out to be quite ordinary and very close to what they'd always told me. Why would they lie over this one detail? I still cared about them enough to believe they would only do that to protect me. But from what? And, in any case, I was old enough now not to need protecting. Wasn't I?

There was only one way to find the answers to these questions, and that was to take Heather's and Seanie's advice. It was time to talk, however painful that might prove to be. Or it would be time in a couple of hours. I reckoned Tom would be at the soccer grounds, and I didn't think it was fair to confront May alone.

I didn't want to meet anyone and have to talk so I got myself out of the Square. I thought about going down to the river again, but it was cold, so instead I wandered up Friary Street. Turning right at the top, I walked along the sweeping crescent of Blackcastle Avenue and passed by the local library building. I decided, for no particular reason, to go inside.

I almost expected to see Heather Kelly at the desk when I came in and drifted down to the Travel section. I picked up a book on Kenya; another one came to hand in the history section. I didn't take them to a table, preferring not to have anyone see what I was reading. I looked up the Samburu in the index of both books and flicked back and forth among the pages.

The Samburu were a wandering, pastoral people from Northern Kenya. The name meant 'butterfly', which seemed right for them. With their slender builds and refined features, one book said, the Samburu appeared delicate, but the impression was deceptive.

There was a photograph of a Samburu girl. She might have passed for my cousin, if not my sister, though her hair was almost completely shaven – unlike my own ragged mop, which I never bothered to do anything different with. Maybe now I will, I thought.

The girl wore a headband of beads and large button-like earrings, not too unlike some of the things May made. Her upper arms and wrists were decorated with a series of tight coils of some white material. She looked very proud and very beautiful, and I felt a kind of pride too at having come from such a people.

It would have been easy to have built up a perfect, rosy picture of some lost paradise I'd missed out on. But the fact was that the Samburu world was, in the end, very much a man's world. Women were good for carrying heavy loads and having lots of children but had no power over their lives.

I left the library more determined than ever to have my questions answered. Down in Friary Sreet again, I passed the Galtee Lounge and remembered the wasted hours I'd spent there with OD and all that hopeful talk of the 'future' I'd bombarded him with, a future I couldn't make him believe in. I thought I'd stopped believing in it myself for what had seemed a very long time. But I remembered what the book said about the Samburu: 'they appear delicate, but the impression is deceptive'. I realised I was strong; stronger and more single-minded than I'd ever imagined.

It had seemed at times as though the future meant nothing to me, but that had never been true. I was back in school only days after giving it up 'forever'; I had taken my own way, not OD's 'drop-out' scheme. And I really was studying, not just pretending. And I wasn't just doing it to get my mind off my troubles. That was rubbish. I'd never had any intention of 'throwing it all away'.

Knowing all this, I felt as ready as I was ever likely to be to face Tom and May. 'Don't let it wait,' I heard Jimmy say all those weeks ago. Ever since Seanie had mentioned that he wasn't well I'd known I had to go and see him. I had another half-hour to spare before Tom got home, I thought, so I went up to De Valera Park. OD would have gone straight to the

MARK O'SULLIVAN

Galtee Lounge once the match was over. When I reached the house the signs weren't good. There was no radio or television noise from inside and, for a few minutes after I knocked at the wreckage of a door, there wasn't even the sound of a footstep. When he finally opened the door I imagined Jimmy had been standing there in the hallway all along, his approach was so silent and unexpected.

I was shocked. His face was sickly and grey – the colour, I thought instinctively, of poverty.

'I'm not feeling the best,' Jimmy said, as if he knew I needed an explanation, as if I deserved one. 'Will you come in?'

The hallway and the kitchen were beginning to look neglected again, but I tried not to let him see I noticed.

'Is it the flu,' I asked, 'or something like that?'

He dropped into his battered armchair by the cold fireplace.

'Naw, I'm just bushed,' he said. 'But I'm still on target. For the old trumpet, you know. I'll have the money together in two weeks.'

He was looking straight at me but his eyes were spinning. I was close enough to have smelled alcohol if he'd been drinking, but he hadn't. I knew there was something badly wrong with him but I couldn't figure out what it could be. All I could think of to do was offer to make some tea.

'Grand,' he said. 'That'd be grand.'

As I searched for some teabags I noticed there was even

147

less food than usual in the presses. In fact, there was nothing that was still edible.

'You need to do some shopping,' I said, only half-joking.

'One of these days,' he answered vaguely. 'We miss having you around, you know.'

'Yeah, right,' I laughed. 'I bet he talks about me all the time.'

'Never a word. That's how I know he misses you – like he misses his mother. He never talks about anything that matters.'

'He never really talked to me either, Jimmy.'

'Yeah, he bottles it all up,' he said. 'And one of these days it's going to blow sky high. I can feel it coming, Nance. Ever since you two split up, I been feeling it.'

I made the tea and thought to myself, *Don't blackmail me, Jimmy, don't pass the blame onto me.* Jimmy, in any case, was busy blaming himself.

'I let him down badly,' he said quietly. 'It's a tough game being a father, or a mother for that matter. No one tells you how to do it right, and you always seem to find out when it's too late.'

I felt like saying that all you had to do was try to be honest, but I didn't believe I had the right to preach.'

'I often look at people like your own mother and father,' he went on. 'Nice, decent people, minding their own business. And they give their kids every chance. What kind of clown am I, Nance? Why couldn't I get it even half-right?'

148

'You shouldn't compare yourself, Jimmy,' I said. 'No one ever gets it right.'

He picked up a matchbox from beside the big gin bottle on the mantelpiece and held it up.

'I don't know much,' he said. 'You could squeeze everything I know into this box and still have room for thirty matches. But I know this much. Tom and May are the salt of the earth. And you're the living proof.'

'Why are you telling me this, Jimmy?'

He grinned wistfully and took a long sip of tea.

'Because I have a notion it's something you don't want to hear. And usually the things you don't want to hear are the things you need to hear.'

Then he laughed out loud and his teeth clicked nervously out of control. 'Did I say that!'

The tension evaporated then and I joined in his laughter – until we heard the front door open. Both of us froze like cats caught dipping into the cream.

OD stood, framed by the kitchen doorway, trying to look cool in the face of the unexpected. I realised I hadn't laid eyes on him for over a month. It hardly seemed possible for two people who'd been living in each other's pockets for so long. And it wasn't as if this was New York or some other big city where there were so many streets to hide in and so many people to hide behind. He hadn't changed much; he was a little untidier maybe, and certainly colder.

'How's the form?' he asked nonchalantly.

'All right,' I said. 'How're you?'

'Yeah, I'm all right too.'

Jimmy struggled to his feet and moved to the door. OD didn't stir and Jimmy had to squeeze past him. He kept staring at me as if his father wasn't even there.

'I'm off for a kip, Nance,' Jimmy called from the hallway. 'See you when I see you, girl.'

'I'd better go too,' I said. OD stood aside to let me pass.

He was still at the kitchen door, staring back inside, when I got to the front door. You won't even try, will you, OD? I thought.

'It didn't work out with Seanie, so?'

'No,' I said, holding the door and not looking back at him.

'Just as well,' he said. 'He's a bastard like his old man.'

I turned slowly and he was turning too. Our eyes met. He looked sad, not hard like the words he'd spat out. I felt myself softening towards him. But not much.

'When are you going to stop feeling sorry for yourself?' I asked him. 'When are you going to get up off your knees and do something better than whinge?'

'Soon. Real soon. You'll see.'

'Yeah, right, and pigs will fly. Look at the way you treat Jimmy just because he's trying to do something. You're afraid he'll succeed and that'll make you an even bigger jerk.'

'Go ahead and slag me off,' he muttered. 'I'm used to it.'

'I couldn't be bothered. I've enough troubles of my own without wasting my time on yours.'

His loud snigger really got my back up. I walked steadily across the hallway and stood within inches of him. It was the closest we'd been for a long time, and the furthest apart.

'Everybody's life is perfect except yours, is that it?' I raged. 'Poor little OD Ryan, the boy the world forgot.'

He was still grinning stupidly so I didn't stop there. I'd wipe that smile off his face no matter what it took.

'Your teachers threw you out of school. Tom wants to throw you off the team. Snipe Doyle treats you like shit.'

'Shut up,' he said.

'Your mammy ran away. Your daddy took back the only pound he ever gave you. Seanie Moran stole your girlfr—'

'Shut up, you black …'

I stepped back to give myself room to swing my arm. He knew it was coming and he didn't try to defend himself. The slap sounded like an explosion; I watched as the faint red outline of my fingers appeared on his pale skin.

'I'm sorry,' he said.

'White trash.'

The hallway seemed longer on the way back to the front door. I slammed the door behind me. It didn't seem possible that the pain could get any worse.

OD

I really blew the big reunion with Nance. There I was at the front door, ready to smash the world to pieces, and as soon as I heard her easy laugh inside, a switch turned in my head. I was all reasonable again, full of good intentions. They didn't last more than a couple of minutes.

She gave me one of those cold, proud looks and I was on the defensive straight away. Everything she said was short and sharp, and then she was heading for the front door and I lost it. That word slipped out and I took what was coming to me. The slap brought me back to that terrible night when Mam and Jimmy laid into each other. By the time she left, I was on for bringing the JCB down to Moran's fancy house and levelling it, never mind finishing off the park.

I changed into a pair of old jeans, flinging stuff all over the place as I charged around my room. When Jimmy called me, I knew why I was making such a racket. I kicked his door open and found him lying on his bed.

'What d'you want?' I asked him gruffly.

'Nance is under pressure,' he said. 'Go after her.'

'We have nothing to say to each other, me and Nance. And anyway, it's none of your business.'

'You might listen for a change. It wouldn't do you any harm.'

I charged over to the bed, caught him by the shirt front and lifted him into a sitting position.

'Don't you tell me what's good for me, Jimmy,' I shouted. 'You lost the right to do that years ago.'

'I know,' he said.

I pulled him closer. His shirt was ripping between my fingers and I grabbed harder.

'I lost my mother because of you.'

'I know.'

I was filling up. The words were catching in my throat. 'We have … we have nothing. We have less than nothing …'

'I know.'

'Stop saying that. Stop saying you know. You know nothing.'

'I –'

'Shut up, Jimmy!' I screamed. 'You bum; you empty, selfish, sick bum. My life is in bits and it's your fault. Everything that's happened to me, all your fault!'

He was looking into my eyes. I realised he was having trouble breathing. I looked down at my hands. They were on his throat. I pushed him away from me and he fell back on the pillow, gasping.

'Brass is back,' he moaned. For a second I thought he was trying to provoke me to finish him off, put him out of his misery. 'Brass is back,' he repeated. With what seemed like his last ounce of strength, he raised himself on one elbow.

I backed away, frightened by what I'd done, terrified by the look on his face.

'Save yourself, OD,' he said in a strangled whisper. 'No one else can do it for you. Save yourself.'

'How?' I said, gagging on the words. 'How the hell can I?'

At the Galtee Lounge, Beano and me got well and truly smashed. At least this time he was drinking before I even got there, but of course I didn't try to stop him. Some of the lads from the team were there waiting for a phone call from the St. Peter's game. We stayed on our own. I couldn't make myself feel excited about the prospect of that call. I was too busy trying to forget what had happened up at the house and building up some Dutch courage for the task ahead.

Beano's big line for the night was another Jack Nicholson – the Joker in *Batman* again: 'You can't make an omelette without breaking some eggs.' He said it so often I asked him if the record was stuck.

Johnny Regan hovered around for a while, but I warned him off. Even when Beano was at the bar getting another round, I was watching.

'What did Johnny say to you?' I asked when he came back.

'Nothing.'

'He was talking to himself, was he?' His eyes were flickering madly, as they always did in the smoky atmosphere of the Galtee.

'You're on about the drugs again, OD,' he said, more loudly than he'd meant to. 'Why do you always treat me like a kid … like I can't think for myself?'

We finished our pints in silence. It was a quarter past nine. Time to make a move.

'Beano,' I said, 'let's go break some eggs.'

I felt a right prat, slipping into that fantasy world where you start to believe that life is a video and you're the star. Then again, a prat is exactly what I was.

For a Saturday night the streets were very quiet and empty. A light drizzle fell, all wispy and shiny under the streetlights. I was pretty steady on my feet but Beano was lurching along in big, wayward strides that took him from one side of the footpath to the other. The sweat was rolling from him and he kept gulping from the big cider bottle in his pocket.

'How did I think of it?' he yelped as we neared the town park.

'Quit the shouting, Beano. And stop drinking that stuff.'

'There's no one around, OD,' he said. 'No one notices the likes of us. Not until now, anyway.'

I was getting nervous and sober, thinking of the consequences of what we were about to do. Next week, I'd be signing on again and looking for a job. Who'd take me on after this escapade? And what if we ended up in court? Then my name would be in the paper and I'd have a criminal record and maybe do some time in jail. I'd have to leave town, and if I started running away at seventeen, where would it end? I'd be just another anonymous loser drifting from town to town, from city to city.

But we were at the park by now and I was already finding reasons for going ahead with our plan. I wasn't going to get a job anyway, criminal record or no criminal record. Not with my address, not with my 'family history'. And in any case, why would I want to hang around this town where I wasn't wanted or respected?

We climbed the gate and ran across to the JCB.

'Did you ever drive anything before?' Beano asked with a wild cackle.

I never had.

'Yeah,' I said. 'I drove Mahoney up the wall.'

He belched out a big, drink-sodden chuckle. His pale face had a queer, ghostly brightness in the faint light. I sensed his strangeness and my bad knee started feeling weak from the running.

We climbed into the cab of the JCB. I searched around for a light but couldn't find any. I was in the driver's seat. Beano was crowding in over my shoulder. My hands were shaking and the keys rattled like chains.

'Get off my back, Beano!'

'Sorry, sorry!'

I was getting used to the dark and starting to see the outline of the dashboard. Eventually, I found the right slot for the key with the tips of my fingers. I slipped the key into place.

'Bingo,' I said. 'We're in business.'

My hand fell on the gearstick and I shoved it forward. We were moving, slowly and jerkily at first, but my aim was true. We were heading for the rockery. The noise in the cab was deafening, the weight on the steering wheel enormous. I couldn't figure out how to move the bucket out front up and down, so I just drove straight into the carefully arranged heap of rocks and clay and plants. We both shot forward and slammed our heads off the windscreen.

My foot was stuck on the accelerator and the JCB inched forward and upwards. We were climbing the rockery and I knew what was at the top end – a drop into the fountain and four feet of water.

I turned the key and pulled it out. The engine went dead. I peered out into the night. We were balanced on top of the rockery and the front wheels couldn't have been more than a few inches from the water in the fountain.

When we moved to jump out, the whole JCB started rocking back and forth. I grabbed Beano's shoulder.

'Take your time,' I said quietly, as if even the sound of my voice might be enough to dump us in the water. 'Open the door real slow and climb down nice and easy, all right?'

Beano's bravado was gone. He whimpered like a child as he

clambered down and the JCB gave a lurch forward. I got to the door and the cab rose, swayed from side to side and dipped again towards the fountain – except this time it didn't stop. I took off like a skydiver without a parachute, and the wet earth came up at me so quickly that I had no chance to stop my fall. My bad knee buckled under me and I screamed out in agony as the JCB plunged, wheels over cab, into the water.

Beano was holding me and screaming something that didn't make sense – until I saw the flashing blue light of a squad car.

'Run for it!' I shouted through my pain. 'Out the back, by the fields. Go on!'

'I can't leave you,' he sniffled. 'I got you into this. I'll take the blame.'

'Go, Beano!'

'No way! No way!'

We were nabbed. The only damage we'd managed to do was to upend the JCB and wreck my knee. It didn't seem worth all the trouble as we sat side by side in the back of the squad car on our way to the Garda barracks. Beano cried all the way.

A couple of young guards took us to a cell. They didn't rough us up or anything, but I still felt like I'd been done over. I made it to the bunk in the corner of the cell. When they locked the door, Beano came and rested his head on my shoulder and I felt his whole body shaking.

'I'm afraid, OD.'

'They'll let us out after a few hours,' I assured him. 'Don't worry.'

That only freaked him out even more. He lay back on the bunk and I saw that his eyes were jammed tight shut. He was gasping for air and I was sure he was going to have some kind of fit. I thought of the drugs again, but I didn't want him to think I didn't believe him – even if he was lying.

'I'm going to die, OD.'

'Cut it out, Beano,' I said, but I was more scared than I'd ever been in my life. I was certain he'd taken something and was just about to call for help when he spoke again.

'You don't understand, OD,' he cried. 'You don't know what it's like to be locked up in a room like this for days … for weeks …'

He opened his eyes and looked around at the walls as if he expected them to cave in at any minute. 'They used to tie me to the bed when they went out. Once they didn't give me anything to eat for three days.'

I held on to him and felt him crumple against me.

'Why did you never tell me, Beano?'

'It was before we met up,' he said. Then he panicked again. 'But it's not like that now, OD. See, it wasn't really anyone's fault. Mammy wasn't well and my father was half-mad from worryin'. But since she got the tablets, things are … grand … they're grand now, honest.'

I didn't have any right to ask him: he was already in bits and he didn't need me to break him up some more. I imagined I was thinking of Beano's welfare, but what was really happening was that I had a new target for my anger. The site foreman from hell. Snipe Doyle.

'What did he do to you that night after the Galtee, Beano?'

He eased himself away from me. There was hate in his eyes and I hoped it wasn't directed at me. I knew I deserved it, the way I was pushing him. Then the smile took root. The Jack Nicholson smile. The one that comes before he gets nasty. Beano was off – as Jack, bawling out Tom Cruise in *A Few Good Men*.

'You can't handle the truth!' he yelled. 'You want the truth? I'll give you the truth!'

'Christ, Beano, give over the play-acting.'

Jack Nicholson disappeared into thin air. Beano's face went dead.

'He pushed me down the stairs,' he said. 'With his fist.'

Behind him, the cell door swung open. The young guard pointed over his shoulder with his thumb.

'Get out of here, lads,' he said. 'There's no charges. Just stay out of trouble or we'll be down on you two like a ton of bricks.'

'But we stole a JCB and we wrecked – ' I began in disbelief.

'Look, we've talked to the Council and to Mr. Moran,' he explained patiently. 'They don't want this story about the park getting out. Bad publicity, you know. Count yourself lucky, lads, and beat it.'

I limped out of the barracks with my arm around Beano

for support. We must have looked like no-hopers in a three-legged race. And no-hopers is what we were. Our big protest had fizzled out, squelched by the powers that be.

At the front gate of our house I said good night to Beano, but I had no intention of going in. A mad idea was brewing in my head. I'd failed to get at Moran or the jerks who let us waste six months on a park that was never to be, but Snipe wouldn't escape my clutches.

'Go home and go to bed, Beano,' I said.

'What if he's there,' he pleaded, 'waiting for me.'

'It's Saturday night, Beano,' I reminded him. 'He'll still be in the pub.'

'I suppose so,' he mumbled dismally and shuffled off. 'You'll still be my pal, won't you, OD?'

It was just what I needed him to say. Now I really could believe I was doing this for him.

'You know I will,' I said. 'Now, go on and go straight to bed, right?'

I pretended to search for my key until I heard the front door of his house close in the distance. My stomach tightened and I looked up at the sky. It had cleared by now. The stars were in their usual places and not taking a blind bit of notice of me. There was a poem in that somewhere, but my mind was far from poetry. I tried putting some weight on the bad leg and it just about held up. That was all right. I wouldn't need to run anyway. I was finished with running, I thought.

Snipe always came home from the pub by a short cut through an alleyway at our end of De Valera Park. All I had to do was get myself over there and wait. I hobbled across the road and into the unlit alleyway. The church bells rang out for midnight and I reckoned on an hour, maybe an hour and a half, before he fell into my trap. I was wrong.

It couldn't have been more than ten minutes before I heard footsteps at the far end of the lane. Snipe had already passed by me before I realised it was actually him. 'You're early,' I called after him.

Snipe wheeled around, but I couldn't see his face well enough to know if he was frightened. I guessed he wouldn't be. In his mind, he was still the tough little scrum-half who wasn't afraid to play a man's game.

'What're you doin' here?'

'I'm waiting for someone,' I said. 'A child abuser. I'm going to give him a taste of his own medicine.'

He sauntered towards me. I could see him better now. His eyelids were half-closed, he wasn't wearing his Rugby Club tie and the buttons of his shirt were open, Mick Moran style.

'You believe that white-headed eejit, do you?'

My fist sank into his beer belly and he keeled over. I kicked him with my good leg until he was flat out on the ground. I gave him one last shot with my bad leg and didn't care about the pain.

'Get up, Snipe. I thought you were supposed to be the hard rugby player.'

He groaned and shuddered uncontrollably. Then he stopped moving.

'Snipe?'

I circled around him, sure he was playing a trick to catch me off my guard. I reached down and twisted his arm behind his back. There was no trick. He was out cold. His breath came in short, wheezy gasps. From the corner of his mouth, a little trail of blood glistened. I didn't know what dying looked like, but I was sure this was it. I panicked and started to run, gripping the wall to hold myself steady.

There'd be no way out of this one if the guards caught me. I had to get out of town, some way or other. I got this lunatic notion of hopping on one of those trains that run through the town at night, down to Cork or up to Dublin. But if I did succeed in reaching either place, I'd need money to get on the boat to England. And I knew where I could lay my hands on some money. It was all madness, but it kept me going.

I had to wait to let a few people pass up the street before I emerged from the alleyway and crossed over to our house. The stairs might as well have been Mount Everest, they took so long to climb. I eased open the door to Jimmy's room. There was just about enough light from the street outside for me to see he was lying facing the window – and to see the big Mexican sombrero on top of the wardrobe.

I had it in my hands when Jimmy stirred and his head turned sharply. He was wide awake. When he saw the sombrero, he looked away again.

'I'm in trouble, Jimmy,' I said, my voice high, not my own, as I stuffed the wad of notes into my pocket. 'I'll send the money back to you.'

He said nothing. He just raised a hand to his mouth, took out his false teeth and dropped them in the glass of water on the bedside table. The water slowly turned red. I scrambled backwards from the room, knowing I was lost, lost forever, and truly sorry that I'd dragged Jimmy down with me. I trundled heavily down the stairs and opened the front door and stood there.

How many times had I wished I'd never have to come back to this house again? I remembered Mam. Had she been thinking what I was thinking now, when she left that last time? That you can't leave fear behind you. That it tags along wherever you go. Maybe that was why she never wrote. I closed out the door behind me – softly.

The railway station was five minutes away if you had two good legs to carry you. It took me twenty minutes. I waited in the shadows for a train I wasn't even sure would stop here.

The tracks leading into the station brought nothing but a raw breeze. I took shelter in a phone booth under the arch of the metal footbridge. After a while, I lifted the receiver and was surprised to find there was a line. When I fished the loose change from my pocket I felt that for once in my life I'd got lucky, but I didn't believe it would last. The clock on the opposite platform said half past twelve. I dialled the first

three digits of Nance's number and stopped. It made no
sense to drag Nance into this. I'd never stopped loving her
and I couldn't let myself hurt her any more than I already
had.

Then I thought I could do one last decent thing before I
escaped or was caught. Snipe was dying up there in a lane in
De Valera Park. He was a bum but no one deserved what I'd
done to him. I'd ring for help. So I rang Dr. Corbett, right?

No, I rang the would-be medical student, Red Cross expert and girlfriend-snatcher himself. I rang Seanie Moran.

NANCE

'It's nearly seven o'clock, Nance,' Tom said accusingly when I came in by the kitchen door. 'We were worried about you, we thought …'

He was sitting at the kitchen table. There was no sign that they'd been eating. This time I hadn't told them where I was going and had made no excuses.

I filled the kettle, bracing myself for the questions I had to ask. Sitting down opposite Tom, I listened to the breathy wail of the boiling water. The memory of that scene with OD brought with it only a dull aching. I felt no emotion. I felt nothing could hurt me more than I was hurt already.

'We've had a phone call,' he said quietly. 'From Heather Kelly.'

I was wrong about the hurt. Betrayal doesn't get any easier to bear.

'She had no right to do that,' I said.

'Maybe not. But she did it for your sake … and for ours.'

I needed to dish out some pain too.

'You dumped her, didn't you?'

'I suppose you could say that,' he admitted, his head bowed. 'So you found a photo of Chris?'

'Yeah, and I had to hear his name from a stranger. Why did she leave the photo there for me to find like that?'

'Nance, I didn't even know she still had it until this afternoon. After Heather rang.'

I was shaken by the way he spoke of the photo, as if it was a secret May had kept from him. 'May's in a pretty bad way,' he said.

'What about me? How do you think I feel?'

'I know, I know … but May is … very disturbed … very …'

I'd never seen him look so utterly defeated. *I'm the one who's been kept in the dark for years*, I thought angrily.

'You're trying to make me feel guilty,' I said. 'You're the ones, you and May, who lied to me.'

Tom sank further down into his chair. Drained of colour, he looked so old it seemed strangely odd that he was wearing a light blue tracksuit.

'If you could just understand, Nance,' he pleaded. 'How young, how naïve we were. I was twenty-three; May was barely twenty-one. We had no plan, no idea how we'd tell you the whole story. We should have … prepared you when you were younger, but … we could never bring ourselves to spoil your childhood.'

'I know all that. I know you didn't mean any harm.'

He brightened a little at that. His smile was grateful.

'Everything we've done has been for your happiness, Nance. We got it badly wrong, but you must believe that.'

'I do,' I said. 'If you just tell me who my mother was, you can pretend I didn't even ask, that I told you everything was all right. I know she's dead and I'm not going to go looking for her family or anything like that. Maybe when I'm older. I have my family, you and May … Was it that American woman in the photo?'

'No,' he said. 'Those damn junkies, they destroyed …'

He buried his head in his hands and his anguish was terrible to see. I eased around the table, afraid but wanting to know who they'd destroyed. I rested my arm on his shoulder as much for my own comfort as for his. It almost seemed like my touch drew the truth from him. But not the truth I expected.

'May is your mother, Nance,' he whispered. 'Your natural mother. Go to her. Please.'

I didn't. I couldn't. Instead, I went to my room and asked myself, over and over again, why she couldn't admit to being my mother. I felt a dread as terrible as my constant nightmare and found myself trying to put American accents on those raised voices I'd so often heard in that dark dream. The accents didn't really fit; but those Americans, I knew, held the key to the mystery of my past.

I heard Tom come quietly up the stairs. He tried both our

doors, mine and May's. They were both locked. He stayed outside on the landing for a long time. I didn't hear him go down, but after a while I was aware that he was gone.

The house was an empty church full of the echoes of nothing. Was it shame, I asked myself? Was that what it came down to? Shame for her half-caste child – me? Was I, after all, someone's 'mistake', not Heather's as I'd thought, but May's? Or was the shame about something else? Something to do with those American junkies, those drug addicts? Had May been involved in all that stuff? It didn't seem possible.

Then the strangest thing happened. I said to myself, *The phone is going to ring* – and it did. I had no idea who it might be, but it didn't matter; I had to get to it first and speak to someone, anyone. Not about my shocking discovery but about anything, something ordinary that could make me believe that life could be normal again in some way.

Only when I reached the phone did it occur to me how late it must be. Tom hadn't appeared and I guessed he'd gone out to escape this place. I wondered if this was Heather Kelly ringing to find out if things had worked out. I let the phone ring a bit longer, hoping it would just stop – the feeling of wanting to talk had gone. The longer it went on, the more urgent the ringing seemed to get. I picked up the phone.

'Nance, it's me. Seanie.'

His voice was quiet, even but insistent. The last thing I needed was complications and I was just about to say so.

'Nance, I got a call from OD. He's at the railway station.

He thinks he might have killed Snipe.'

The first foolish thought I had was that OD hadn't rung me. Then the word 'killed' hit me. I wanted to scream 'No!'

'Will you come to the station with me?' he asked.

OD had always been so near the edge, I shouldn't have been so shocked. Had I pushed him over the edge with that slap in the face? Please, I thought, don't let it be my fault. Please, don't let it be true that Snipe is dead.

'Look, Nance, I have to go. Every second counts. Are you coming or not?'

'Yeah,' I said. 'Yeah. I'll come.'

The line went dead. I put the phone down. I grabbed a coat and scarf. I went out the back door so May wouldn't hear the front door close. If it even mattered to her any more. I'd almost turned the corner into the drive when I saw Tom lying on one of the white plastic garden chairs out in the middle of the back lawn. I moved across the wet grass towards him.

In spite of the cold, he'd fallen asleep. I supposed that he hadn't slept for such a long time that the weight of tiredness had brought him down. I slipped off my coat and placed it lightly over him. When I turned to take a last look at him, I saw that it was May's coat I'd put on without knowing. Her scarf too. I left the scarf on. I needed it.

Back in the house, I got myself another jacket, one of my own cord ones. When I reached the front gate, Seanie was pulling up in the Morris Minor. All I could think of to say was, 'Why did he ring you, Seanie?'

'I don't know, Nance,' he said. 'I can't figure it out. But he sounded bad, really bad. I just hope he's still ... he's still there when we ...'

I knew what he was saying and I thought angrily, it would be just like OD to act the dumb martyr and wait for the train on the tracks and not think what that might do to the rest of us.

It didn't take long for us to reach the railway station. I can't say I was afraid, at least not for myself. I was too numb.

OD sat stiffly upright on a bench at the station platform, like a blind man who's got day and night confused and waits for a train that will never come. I was sure he hadn't seen us through his trance, but when we got to within a few feet of him, I knew that his eyes had followed us all the way down the platform. He lowered them then.

Of the three of us only Seanie could think clearly enough to speak.

'Where's Snipe?' he asked OD.

'In the alley opposite our house.'

'Come on then, we'd better hurry,' Seanie said. OD still hadn't looked up from the brick-paved platform.

'You go,' OD said. 'I'm waiting for the train.' Seeing that old melodramatic self-pity in him again, I exploded.

'You've never faced up to anything in your life, OD,' I snapped. 'Why start now? Come on, Seanie.'

But Seanie wasn't following orders. He took hold of OD's arm and lifted him from the bench. OD stared at him and I waited for a fight to break out.

'I can't walk,' OD said helplessly. 'My knee's gone.'

'You got as far as here, OD,' Seanie told him. "You can walk to the car.'

Seanie turned away and went past me. OD followed him, dragging his bad leg like a punishment. I followed OD and we piled into the Morris Minor – OD in the back, on his own.

As Seanie drove us to De Valera Park, OD told us calmly, with no hint of justifying his savagery, why he'd beaten up Snipe. If Seanie and I had been his trial jury, OD would have got off. Even as I thought this, I knew it meant I was accepting something I never imagined I could accept. That violence isn't always unjustifiable. It was a frightening and dangerous conclusion and OD himself couldn't agree with it.

'It was wrong, full stop,' he said. 'And it gets worse … what I did to Jimmy.'

I thought nothing he could say would shock me, until he told us about stealing Jimmy's money and about that awful bloom of red in the glass of water. The jury was out again on OD.

We got to the entrance of the alleyway. As Seanie opened the driver's door, OD said to me, not seeming to care that Seanie could hear, 'You'll hate me now. You'll always hate me once you've seen what I did.'

Seanie helped OD out of the car and we passed from the yellow light of the street to the near-darkness of the alleyway.

'Give him a hand, Nance,' Seanie said. 'I'll go up ahead.'

I put my arm around OD's waist and felt him trembling. How many times had we stood in that alleyway, holding each other? How could we ever have imagined as we kissed that it would come to this?

'He's behind Donovans',' OD called in a stifled whisper after Seanie.

I knew Donovans' back wall because we'd often had a laugh over the message sprayed in pink lettering there. 'Jim Donovan is a dennsser, Sined Larry Donovan.' It didn't seem very funny any more.

Seanie moved forward beyond the turn in the alley and OD faltered so that I had to make a greater effort to hold on to him. It was already a big effort because somehow I felt it wasn't OD I was holding.

Seanie was back in seconds flat.

'He's not there,' he said.

'Are you sure?'

OD pulled away from me and stared in disbelief along the alleyway.

'They've already found him, the guards,' he cried. 'What do I do now?'

'If they found him and he was … if it was serious, the place would be cordoned off,' Seanie said. 'He must have made it home. Or someone else found him.'

'Beano!' OD and I said at the same time.

All at once the tautness in OD, the clenched fists, the grinding jaws, relaxed. He looked like the OD I preferred to remember, the one I imagined had gone forever: easy in himself, that cool trace of smiling optimism back in place.

'I'm going over to Snipe's to see if he's all right,' he said. 'Then I'm giving myself up. It's what I have to do, isn't it, Nance? Isn't it, Seanie?'

'Yeah,' Seanie agreed. 'But I don't have the right to say.'

'You didn't, Seanie, but you do now,' OD said. 'Will you do me one last favour? Bring me to the barracks after I talk to Beano?'

'Sure.'

We helped him across the street and down towards Snipe's house. My arm was still around his waist and he felt warmer, softer. When I had to let him go at the gate, I thought I was going to fold up. I thought of Jimmy and saved myself.

'What about Jimmy?' I asked.

'Jimmy's better off without me,' OD answered. 'Will you help him get his trumpet, Nance? Make sure he gets it, won't you?'

'Course I will,' I said, though it was clear to me that if OD was sent to prison, there would be no trumpet. Jimmy was never buying the trumpet for himself. He was doing it for OD, to prove there was a way back no matter how far you'd fallen.

'That letter you sent me,' OD said. 'You never told me what you had to sort out. Not that I had the cop-on to ask. Did you sort it out?'

'Not yet,' I had to admit. But he had enough to feel bad

about, why burden him with more? 'We'll talk about it ... later.'

He leaned against the pier of the gate to get the weight off his leg and drew me towards him slowly, afraid I'd resist.

'I hope there's time to talk,' he said and kissed my forehead lightly.

I noticed a light come on behind closed curtains in an upstairs room of the house. I was certain it was Snipe's shadow I saw move across behind it, but I didn't say anything about it. I didn't want to raise OD's hopes. The monster in him still haunted me and I couldn't respond to his kiss. I knew he understood. He smiled sadly. He looked from me to Seanie and back again.

'Nance, you two should ... you'd be good for each other.'

'Don't be daft, OD,' Seanie said. 'She never stopped going out with you.'

He wasn't angry. He was like the old Seanie we knew from school, stating facts in a detached, unemotional way.

'Tell him, Nance,' he went on. 'You know it's true. And that's fine with me because ...'

OD was looking bewildered – looking like I felt.

'I can't ... after everything you did for me,' I said. 'I know you wanted to go out with me and I threw it all back in your face.'

OD was like a spectator at a tennis match. He turned to Seanie.

'I never wanted to go out with you, Nance,' Seanie said.

'I tried to explain it once but ...'

Two words from Seanie, more like a sigh of relief, and we were left breathless.

'I'm gay.'

He smiled. I thought he was going to laugh.

'I never told anyone before.'

'But you play football ... you're ...' OD stammered.

'I wouldn't be the first queer to play football, OD.'

I felt cheated in some stupid way, embarrassed at the presumptions I'd made about him and me. But I was impressed too, by his honesty, his courage.

'So, what was all that stuff about between us?' I asked.

He shrugged his shoulders. 'I needed a friend. You needed a friend.' He turned to OD. 'Look, you'd better go in. We'll wait in the car ... That is, if you don't mind, Nance.'

'Don't be silly,' I said.

We walked back to the car as OD hobbled in along the path to the house. I told Seanie who my mother was. I thought he deserved to know, and I knew my secret was safe with him. He was used to secrets.

He said, 'Nance, let's make a pact.'

I agreed. He was going to go to his parents and talk. I was going to go to May. And listen.

OD

How could I have expected that Beano wouldn't have changed towards me? As he came through the hallway, I still clung to that foolish hope. One look into those angry eyes rubbished all hope. Of course, I knew he would never understand why I'd hammered his father; but it was worse than that. He had seen through my guise of friendship and recognised it for what it was. Pity, the worst form of charity.

'I'm sorry,' I said.

'Leave us alone.'

'I was so mad over what he did to you, Beano. I know it's no excuse but – '

'You beat up my father because you hate everyone, 'cause you think it's all their fault you ended up a nobody. Like me.'

'You're not – '

'I don't need you to tell me what I am,' he shouted into the night. 'You're not my friend, you never were. You thought you were some kind of babysitter or something.

Well, I don't need no babysitter.'

There was no Jack Nicholson, no mixed-up, borrowed lines. This was the real Beano. A total stranger to me.

'Is he all right?' I asked. 'Your old … your father?'

'He'll be fine,' Beano said. 'You're not half as tough as you think you are.'

'I know, Beano, but Seanie is with me. If there's any cuts or anything, he could fix him up.'

'Clear off, the lot of you,' he said, getting agitated again. 'We don't need anyone. We stick together. Us Doyles.'

The light from the bare bulb in the hallway shone through his wild, white, wispy hair. It was like a halo above his unearthly face. Glowing before me, this strange, unforgiving angel answered my miserable protests with a cruel clarity.

'But you can't let him do these things to you.'

'I have a choice, do I?' he said. 'You see how people look at me, how they try to make a feck of me. Did you ever see me with a girl, did you? What girl would bother with a little scut like me? I have no one, only my father and Mammy. All the rest of ye, ye'll go yer own way. That leaves me … and them. They're all I have.'

'I'm giving myself up, Beano,' I said, trying to be a hero, making the big sacrifice for him, for my friend. 'I'm going down to the barracks now.'

'Don't waste your time,' he told me. 'My father fell on the way home from the pub, that's all. Right there at the gate. I saw him falling 'cause I was waiting here at the door for him.'

'Beano! He told you to say this just to protect himself.'

'Naw, I saw it with my own eyes.'

'Beano, I won't let you do this,' I said. 'I'm going to the guards and telling them the truth about me and about what Snipe did to you.'

'I made all that up … after you gave me the drugs, OD. That's what I'll tell the guards if you grass on my father.'

'Beano, please …'

'Don't bother calling up again, OD,' he said as he closed the door. 'You think this is all his idea, don't you? Poor dumb Beano couldn't work out a deal like this.'

I backed away from the door. I was free again but it didn't feel like that. I limped over towards the car, making myself suffer, banging my foot on to the ground to feel the slicing pain shudder through my knee. The pain didn't hide the agony of what I was thinking.

Would Jimmy reject me too? Would he ignore my apologies and excuses with the same bitter finality that Beano had shown? I thought I couldn't go on. Surrender would have been easier.

Seanie rolled down the window of the car. They were both peering out at me like I was a drowning man. I told them about Beano's deal. After that there wasn't much more to say. I was thinking about Jimmy and getting more and more afraid of facing him.

'Will ye come up for a cup of tea or …?' I asked.

My voice cracked. Don't break now, I screamed at myself.

Then there was an answering echo. For once in your life, it said, be honest and take the hand they're holding out to you.

'I can't go in to Jimmy on my own,' I admitted. 'Five minutes?'

When we went inside, I was suddenly aware of the wad of notes deep in my pocket, digging into my thigh. I pulled it out and stared at the evidence of my awful crime. The notes fell open and what I saw made me want to throw up. Among the crisp fivers and tenners was the brown envelope with my poem written on it. The pencil marks were already fading, but below the four lines Jimmy had scrawled, with a dodgy biro, my name and the date I'd written the poem.

'What's that?' Nance asked. I tightened my grip around the envelope.

'Something I wrote,' I said. 'I can't believe he kept it. I threw it in the fireplace after I finished it. I thought he dumped it with the ashes.'

'A poem?'

'Yeah. He should've dumped it. It's crap.'

'Can I see it?'

I handed over the envelope and she read through my words a couple of times. Then, to my astonishment, she read the poem aloud. It seemed to become something new when she read it. I heard a music, a rhythm I didn't realise was there.

> *Joining hands with the Glass Druid,*
> *Calling to the standing stones,*

The men and women who can't speak to me;
Voices like mine, without sounds, without tones.

She made to give the tattered envelope back to me. 'I don't want the stupid thing,' I said, although it wasn't true.

'It's good, it really is,' she told me.

'It's nothing but self-pity,' I said. 'Me, me, me.'

'It's about all of us,' Seanie said. 'I wish I could write like that.'

Hope was pouring back in great waves and I started thinking, Yes, I can do this!

Maybe I didn't get it exactly right with that poem; but, in a way, it was right for when I wrote it. And if I could get that much right, what was to stop me getting the rest of my life right?

'I'll put on the kettle and tell Jimmy I'm back,' I said. 'Just wait 'til I get this over with, all right?'

'I'll make the tea,' Nance said. 'You go ahead.'

In spite of the aching knee, my step was light on the stairs. I was like a child running to his father with some prize he'd just won. His door was still wide open from my earlier, hasty exit. His face was turned, as always, to the wall. He seemed so deep in sleep that I hesitated to wake him. Then I decided I had to: I knew he never wanted to wake up again, and I knew that was my fault.

I shook his shoulder lightly.

'Jimmy,' I whispered, 'I brought back the money. Everything's sorted out, Jimmy.'

I gave him time. I tried not to be angry, not to think that he was just pretending to be asleep to escape talking to me, but still he didn't wake up. Then I leaned in over him to see if his eyelids were flickering. Soon as I saw how his jaw hung so slackly, I knew something was badly wrong. I took his head between my hands and moved it gently towards me. The unshaven cheeks were rough against my palms. A sound somewhere between a sigh and a moan escaped his lips. I let go of him and his head fell back on the pillow.

When I tried to call out the first time, nothing came. I gasped for air. I turned for the door and my knee gave way. I hit the floor and dragged a scream from the pit of my stomach.

'Nance! Seanie!'

They found me crawling across the floor. Nance switched on the light and I was blinded for a moment. When I opened my eyes, Seanie was by Jimmy's side. He raised Jimmy and I saw, in the brutal light, the face of an old, old man.

'He's going to die,' I cried. 'And he'll never know I came back.'

'Nance, get a doctor,' Seanie said. 'And an ambulance. It's his heart.'

Seanie was kneeling on the bed and ripping the pyjama top from Jimmy's chest. I couldn't take any more. On all fours, I got myself onto the landing. I was wailing, screaming, begging for forgiveness, beating my head against the wall, telling Jimmy I'd get his trumpet, pleading with him not to go.

Then the house came alive with people rushing up and down the stairs and Nance picked me up from the landing floor, where I'd rolled myself into a ball in the corner.

'He's going to be all right, OD,' she said. 'You'll have to go in the ambulance with him.'

I was like a zombie. I couldn't talk. All I could do was follow her down the steps. Seanie was at the door, his hair wet with sweat. I grabbed his hand. It was all I could do to thank him. Nance brought me out to the ambulance; as I climbed in, she said, 'When you get home, call up to my house. No matter how late it is, right?' Through the wash of my tears she seemed to be fading away.

'Seanie was right,' she said. 'I never stopped loving you. Maybe – '

A nurse rushed up the steps into the ambulance beside me and pulled in the doors. I talked to Jimmy all the way over, even though he was unconscious and covered with an oxygen mask. Maybe the nurse thought I was mad, but I'm sure she'd seen it all before. Plans for him, plans for me. Getting his trumpet, finding a bunch of old rockers like himself, going on the road again – 'no drink, mind, Jimmy!' – and some new gear – 'maybe even a black velvet suit, what do you think, Jimmy?' And me. Back to the books, to school, keep the head down, and writing – 'I'm no Dylan Thomas, but I have something, I know it, Jimmy! Seanie said it, Nance said it.' Nance – 'Could it be, Jimmy? Could we start over, me and Nance? Me and you?'

183

I tried so hard but I still believed it was all my fault. Until some time, hours later, when the sky outside the hospital waiting room was already brightening and a white-coated doctor came and asked me a whole bunch of questions about Jimmy. At first I was angry with him because my lack of answers showed me how little I'd cared about Jimmy this last while.

'When was the last time your father drank alcohol? Did he eat regularly? Did you notice any disorientation? His balance, his ...'

'Yeah, yeah, I did,' I said. 'So? Why are you asking me all these things? Is it serious or not?'

The doctor, a young man, had probably seen it all too. He waited for me to calm down before he went on.

'Your father is going to be fine, thanks to that young chap – Sean, is it?' he said. 'I'm trying to confirm the diagnosis, the reasons why your father suffered this ... this trauma.'

I hid my face from him.

'I know why. I did it to him. I –'

'Your father's heart attack was brought on by malnutrition. I'm wondering why ... why he might have stopped eating. We can't find a physical reason.'

Malnutrition! The word didn't seem to belong at the end of the twentieth century, not in Ireland, not unless you had a cause like Bobby Sands had, not for a damned trumpet. Then I knew that sometimes even a knocked-up trumpet is worth going to the edge for. It was with a strange mixture of relief and deep, deep sadness that I looked up at him.

'For a trumpet. For me.'

At around seven in the morning, the hospital came to life slowly with the rattle of trolleys and the squeak of nurses' rubber soles reverberating in the big green-painted corridors. They brought me some tea and toast but I couldn't touch the toast. I asked for a phone and just after eight I rang Seanie's house to thank him properly. He answered quickly but his voice seemed tired.

'OD here,' I said. 'Did I wake you?'

'We haven't been to bed,' he said. 'How's Jimmy?'

'They haven't let me see him yet but he's fine, they said. If it hadn't been for you, Seanie …'

Then it twigged with me what he'd just said about not getting to bed.

'You've been talking to your folks? About … about it.'

'Yeah, I tried anyway.'

'It didn't go too well?'

'You could say that.'

I didn't know what to tell him. The whole thing was too strange to me; and to be honest, in spite of what he'd done for Jimmy, I felt uncomfortable even talking to him. Which was totally out of line. He deserved better and I knew it.

'Seanie? Remember the poem I wrote?' I said, 'Well, there's a second verse. And the standing stones learn to speak. Some of them, anyway.'

'I hope you're right, OD,' he said.

'I hope so too, Seanie.'

'By the way, St. Peter's lost their game. We won the League.'

It didn't seem to matter much. Not to him, not to me. I didn't have long more to wait to see Jimmy. At the door of the Intensive Care ward, the nurse whispered, 'Five minutes. We don't want to tire him out.' I opened the door and went inside. To my father.

NANCE

I opened the door and went inside. To my mother. The unlocked door seemed to offer the possibility of a new beginning. But not until I'd heard the end of our story and the silence between us was over. Her room was colder than the street outside. In the small light from the bedside lamp I could see that her dark hair was a mess and her eyes were red and heavy. I thought about sitting on the bed but, instead, I sat on the chair alongside it. She was looking up at me like a small animal whose trapper has come to finish her off.

From downstairs, I heard the unexpected noises of Tom pottering about. I hadn't seen him when I came in and thought he'd gone to bed in the spare room. I heard the loud rushing sound of the central heating coming on and I knew that whatever happened between May and me in the next while, he was determined to get things back to normal in our house again. The clatter of pans and crockery from the

187

kitchen confirmed that feeling. He couldn't have known how wonderful those ordinary sounds seemed to me – even if it was the middle of the night.

'You'll always hate me now, Nance,' May said. I was taken aback at hearing her echo OD's words.

'No, I won't,' I assured her. 'I just want to understand why you didn't tell me. Or why Tom didn't.'

May sat up warily, raised her knees and wrapped her arms tightly around them.

'It's not Tom's fault,' she said. 'He wanted to tell you long ago but I wouldn't let him. I thought, if I could carry this … this burden for you, then you'd get by without ever having to know. You must believe me, Nance, I'd make any sacrifice for you, even denying I was your natural mother.'

She squeezed her arms tighter about her knees and then released her grip. She leaned back on the pillows.

'It seems so stupid now. I know it probably won't even make sense to you. I was afraid of what other people would think of me, of what my mother would have thought of me if she'd ever known.'

I'd never met her mother. She'd died shortly after May and Tom came back from Kenya. She didn't talk about her very much but when she did, it was always with a sadness I thought I understood.

'I was all ready to tell her everything. But when we got back home she was dying from cancer. Tom pushed me to do it, almost too hard. We very nearly split up over it. When my mother died and I hadn't told her, I felt I could never tell anyone.'

'Tell me about Chris,' I said, trying hard not to feel bad about being seen as just 'anyone'.

She swallowed a mouthful of air and her eyelids trembled as she struggled to form words.

'Nance, it wasn't anything to do with the fact that … that I'd had a child before I married or that your father was black. It wasn't those things at all. Chris was a good man, really. He just went wrong, awfully wrong.'

The radiator was knocking and the room was heating up. But the chill was still seeping into my bones. I had never felt so cold. What she said next sounded as if she'd rehearsed it during those long days when we weren't talking to each other. There was no confused rambling or uncertainty. She told her story as precisely as she painted her watercolours, but she had never painted a landscape as harshly realistic as this.

'We had been going out just two months when I got pregnant. Soon as we found out, we knew we'd have to leave our teaching jobs in Nairobi, that's how it was then. But we were going to get married and he was looking for a job up north. At least, I thought he was. But after you were born he'd appear for a day or two and then he'd be gone. It didn't take long for me to realise what was wrong. I'd seen the signs when I worked a summer in the States in '76. We argued and he left. I thought I'd never see him again. Oh, God!'

'He was on drugs?' I gasped. 'Those Americans in the photo …?'

'They came along just when Chris was at his lowest. He couldn't get a job and some of his family were giving him a hard time over me. Annie and Doug, they were touring Africa – or touring the drug scene of Africa, more like. They ended up in Morocco, but not before they destroyed Chris.'

Her hand reached for the bedside lamp and she switched it off. Even though the curtains were open, it took some time before I could begin to see the outline of her face again. In all that time, she never spoke. Below us, Tom was still busy, but I wondered if there was any point. And, in my mind, I was making some kind of connection between Chris and OD – a connection I didn't like. Her voice surprised me in the dark because it had become stronger.

'Months passed and Chris never showed,' she said. 'I was completely lost. I'd no idea what I was going to do. Heather put us up and fed us. Then Tom arrived on the scene. He and Heather were at the same school and they started going out. We, you and I, we moved to Mombasa. I'd got a secretarial job there. But it was hotter there, more humid, and you were always sick. Eventually the company gave me a job in Nairobi and we went back. Then I got to know Tom.'

It was becoming more and more painful for her, but I was afraid to move closer. The rhythm of her speech slowed like a train when it approaches its station.

'We seemed to click straight off. It wasn't a question of me setting out to steal him from her. We were just right for each other and Heather knew it. She was furious, and I couldn't blame her. I even tried to break it off with Tom, but he wouldn't have it. He went to the airport the night Heather was leaving but she wouldn't talk to him. That was the night it all happened … the worst night of our lives. A nightmare, Nance, a nightmare.'

She paused. The train had reached its destination. A place darker than the room we were in.

'Even as I let Chris in to the house I knew there was going to be trouble. His eyes were dead and wild at the same time. He wanted to see you. You'd just started walking and you were under the table playing some little game.'

It was a nightmare all right. My nightmare. And my nightmare was true. It might have been someone else's story now, she sounded so detached. I suppose it was the only way she could get through the hard bit.

'We screamed and shouted at each other for I don't know how long, and then the door crashed open. It was Tom.'

It all made sense now, all those terrifying noises in my dream. I began to sweat as heavily as I did when that dream came, but I couldn't stir myself to take off my coat and scarf.

'Tom got him out to the landing, but Chris got the better of him and pushed him over the stair rails. He broke his femur, that's why he has that limp. Chris was driving away

191

from Nairobi when the car crashed. It was instant, they told us; he didn't have to suffer any more.'

My father, a junkie, almost a murderer. I was devastated. I felt unclean. I felt like a stone. May was crying again.

'Nance, I'll never forget poor Chris's face before he ran. It was the old Chris, the real Chris. He looked like he'd woken from a nightmare and couldn't understand what had happened to him, what he'd done. He was in such pain, he was suffering so much I was glad … it's a terrible thing to say … but I was glad his life ended then, that his suffering was over.'

'Why did you keep the photo, May?' I asked.

'Because that was the last good day we had together, the last day of our … love.'

May folded up then. She was so small and vulnerable, under the bedcovers, that I couldn't bear it. I went to the bed and, with a huge effort – part of me hated her for destroying the father in my mind and part of me loved her for loving him – I held on to her.

We stayed that way for so long that my arm, cradling her head, went numb and when Tom came upstairs and tapped lightly on the door, I was glad. For the first time in weeks, we were together. I told them about Jimmy but I left out the rest. That was OD's business, OD's wreckage, OD's secret. We had ours. Some day maybe they'd know, but not now. Though I knew it wasn't going to be easy to live with what I knew, I was happy to have my family back again. And OD.

Yes, OD had gone some way along that road that had led Chris to his doom, but he'd crawled from the wreckage. The road goes on to a place beyond the wreckage and if OD stayed on that road, I'd walk with him.

There would be worlds for us to discover out there. New worlds, old worlds, the world of Kenya and the Samburu among them – not a perfect world but nonetheless part of what I am. May and Tom, for reasons that were in the end unselfish, had kept that world from me; but I'd kept myself from it too, for too long. Now I was hungry for knowledge of it and hungry for the future.

Morning came and we let the new day settle in for a while before we moved on. Tom went downstairs to cook us a fry. The smell of rashers, sausages and eggs filled the house and the sound of a Sunday morning radio blasted us back to normality. Then the front doorbell rang. It was OD. Tom must have known because he let me answer it.

'He's going to make it, Nance,' OD said.

'I'm glad.'

We stood staring at each other. I knew he'd been up all night too but he looked rested, easy. Behind me, Tom emerged from the kitchen, his sleeves rolled up, his face red and healthy from the heat of the kitchen.

'I'm doing breakfast for the ladies, OD,' he said. 'Would you care to join us?'

OD glanced uncertainly at me. Then he smiled.

'Yeah,' he said. 'If you only knew how hungry I am!'